THE
ICE
MONSTER

D1343450

Previously written by David Walliams:

THE BOY IN THE DRESS
MR STINK
BILLIONAIRE BOY
GANGSTA GRANNY
RATBURGER
DEMON DENTIST
AWFUL AUNTIE
GRANDPA'S GREAT ESCAPE
THE MIDNIGHT GANG
BAD DAD

THE WORLD'S WORST CHILDREN
THE WORLD'S WORST CHILDREN 2
THE WORLD'S WORST CHILDREN 3

Also available in picture book:

THE SLIGHTLY ANNOYING ELEPHANT
THE FIRST HIPPO ON THE MOON
THE QUEEN'S ORANG-UTAN
THE BEAR WHO WENT BOO!
THERE'S A SNAKE IN MY SCHOOL!
BOOGIE BEAR
GERONIMO

David Walliams

THE ICE MONSTER

Illustrated by Tony Ross

HarperCollins *Children's Books*

First published in Great Britain by
HarperCollins *Children's Books* in 2018
HarperCollins *Children's Books* is a division of HarperCollins*Publishers* Ltd,
HarperCollins Publishers
1 London Bridge Street
London SE1 9GF

The HarperCollins website address is:
www.harpercollins.co.uk

2 4 6 8 10 9 7 5 3

Text copyright © David Walliams 2018
Illustrations copyright © Tony Ross 2018
Cover lettering of author's name copyright © Quentin Blake 2010
All rights reserved.

ISBN 978–0–00–832405–6

CHILDREN'S FICTION / HUMOUR

David Walliams and Tony Ross assert the moral right to be
identified as the author and illustrator of the work respectively.

This is a work of fiction. Names, characters, businesses, places, events, locales and
incidents are either the products of the author's imagination or used in a fictitious
manner. Apart from famous historical figures, any resemblance to actual persons,
living or dead, or actual events is purely coincidental.

A CIP catalogue record for this title is available from the British Library.

Printed and bound in India by Thomson Press India Ltd.

Conditions of Sale
This book is sold subject to the condition that it shall not,
by way of trade or otherwise, be lent, re-sold, hired out or otherwise
circulated without the publisher's prior consent in any form, binding or cover other
than that in which it is published and without a similar condition
including this condition being imposed on the subsequent purchaser.

This book is produced from independently certified FSC® paper
to ensure responsible forest management.

For Alfred.
You are always in my heart.
Daddy x

THANK-YOUS

I WOULD LIKE TO THANK:

MARKETUS ANDUS
PR DIRECTORUM
Geraldine Stroud

EDITORIUS III
Alice Blacker

BIGGUS BOSSIUS
Charlie Redmayne

AGENTUS LITERATI
Paul Stevens

ILLUSTRATORUS
MAGNIFICUS
Tony Ross

EXECUTIVIS PUBLISHERARIUS
Ann-Janine Murtagh

PUBLISHARUM
Rachel Denwood

PUBLISHUS DIRECTORUS
Kate Burns

PUBLISHUS DIRECTORUS
Harriet Wilson

MANAGERUM EDITORIUS
Samantha Stewart

CREATIVUS DIRECTORUS
Val Brathwaite

ARTIUS FARTIUS
Sally Griffin

DESIGNUM
Matthew Kelly

ARTIUS DIRECTORUS
David McDougall

DESIGNUM
Elorine Grant

DESIGNUM
Kate Clarke

AUDIUS BOOKIUS
Tanya Hougham

NATURAL HISTORY MUSEUM

The year is 1899

and we're in Victorian London. Meet the characters in the story...

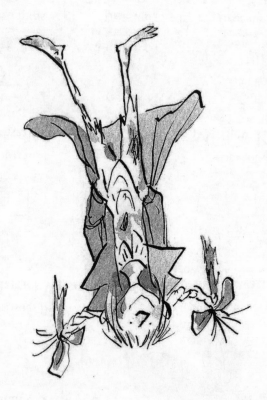

Elsie is a homeless orphan, who lives on the streets of London.

Dotty is the cleaning lady at the Natural History Museum. She is as daft as her brushes.

Private Thomas is Dotty's boyfriend, the shortest soldier who ever served in the British Army. His fellow soldiers call him "Titch". He is now retired, and lives at the Royal Hospital Chelsea, making him a "Chelsea Pensioner".

Commissioner Barker is the fearsome head of the London Metropolitan Police, famous for his tiny moustache.

Mr Clout is the brute of a security guard at the museum, infamous for his hobnailed boots.

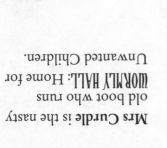

Mrs Curdle is the nasty old boot who runs WORMLY HALL: Home for Unwanted Children.

Many years ago, the **Professor** was the top scientist at the museum, until one of his experiments went catastrophically wrong.

Lady Buckshot is an aristocratic big-game hunter. Across Africa she shoots elephants, giraffes and lions and brings their bodies back to the museum to be stuffed and put on display.

The **admiral** is the only sailor to live at the hospital. He was thrown out of the old sailors' home for being drunk and disorderly.

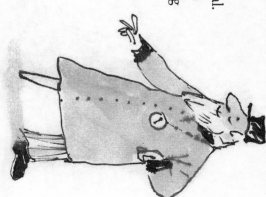

The **colonel** and the **brigadier** are also Chelsea Pensioners.

The one-eyed **sergeant major** is in charge of everyone and everything that comes in and out of the hospital, and don't you forget it.

All the Chelsea Pensioners are overseen by the Royal Hospital's formidable **Matron**.

Abdul Karim is always at the Queen's side. He is her handsome young Indian attendant, also known as "Munshi".

Queen Victoria is the ruler of the British Empire. In 1899, she had been on the throne for what was the longest reign in British history, a staggering sixty-two years.

Sir Ray Lankester is the museum's portly director.

The **sandwich-board man** roams the streets, trying to convince everyone that "THE END IS NIGH".

The **captain** is in charge of what was, in 1899, one of the Royal Navy's most modern warships, HMS *Argonaut*.

The Sticky Fingers Gang is a rough and tough band of child robbers, who are infamous for being the greatest thieves in London.

Raj the First has his own confectionery emporium – or sweet trolley.

And last, but certainly not least…

...is the **ICE MONSTER** itself, a woolly mammoth that died ten thousand years ago. The lifeless animal was discovered by Arctic explorers, perfectly preserved in the ice.

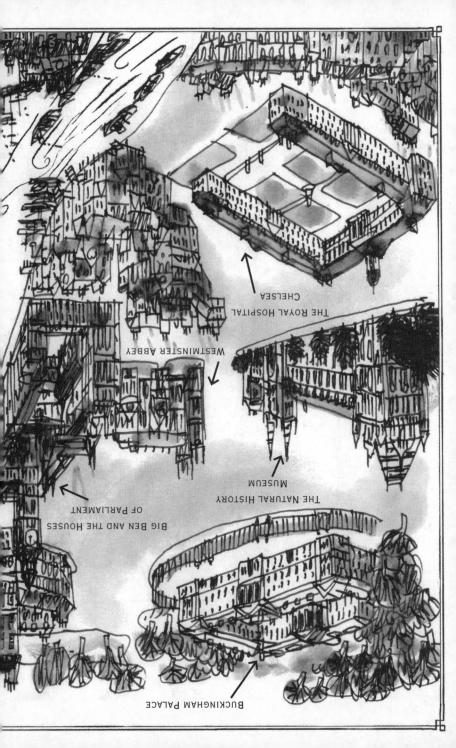

THE ROYAL HOSPITAL
CHELSEA

WESTMINSTER ABBEY

THE NATURAL HISTORY
MUSEUM

BIG BEN AND THE HOUSES
OF PARLIAMENT

BUCKINGHAM PALACE

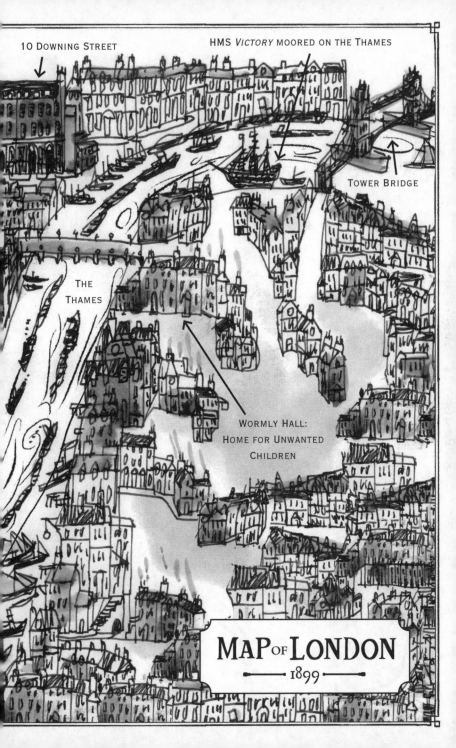

10 DOWNING STREET

HMS *VICTORY* MOORED ON THE THAMES

TOWER BRIDGE

THE THAMES

WORMLY HALL:
HOME FOR UNWANTED
CHILDREN

MAP OF LONDON
1899

PART I
LONDON
1899

Chapter 1

COCKROACHES
FOR BREAKFAST

One bleak winter night, in the back streets of London, a tiny baby was left on the steps of an orphanage. There was no note, no name, no clue as to who this little person was. Just the potato sack in which she was wrapped, as snow fell around her.

In Victorian times, it was not uncommon for newborn babies to be abandoned outside orphanages, hospitals or even the homes of upper-class folk. Their poor, desperate mothers hoped their children would be taken in and given a better life than their birth families could provide.

However, it was hard to imagine a WORSE start
in life for this baby than at WORMLY HALL, Home for
Unwanted Children.

Twenty-six orphans lived there, all crammed into a room that should have slept eight at the absolute most. The children were locked up, starved and beaten. On top of that, they were forced to work day and night. They had to assemble gentlemen's pocket watches from tiny pieces until they went blind.

All the children were painfully thin, with filthy rags for clothes. The orphans' faces were black with soot, so all you could see in the gloom were their hopeful little eyes.

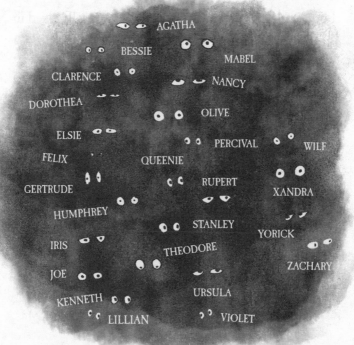

When a new baby arrived at the orphanage, all the older children would come up with a name for them. They liked to work their way through the alphabet so their names would be as different as possible. The night the baby in the potato sack was left on the steps, they had reached E. If she had been found the day before, she might have been called "Doris". A day later, she could have been a "Frank". Instead, she was named **"Elsie"**.

This prison of an orphanage was run by an **evil** old boot named Mrs Curdle. Her face was usually fixed in a permanent grimace, and she was covered from head to toe in warts. She had so many warts even her warts had warts. The only thing that made her smile was the sound of children sobbing.

Mrs Curdle would scoff all the food donated for the orphans, so the children in her care had to eat cockroaches for breakfast, lunch and dinner.

"Creepy-crawlies are good for you!" she would chuckle.

If any of the orphans spoke after "candles out",

she would stuff one of her pus-sodden old stockings in their mouth. They would have to keep it there for a week.

"That'll keep you quiet, windy wallet!"

When the children were sleeping on the cold stone floor, she would put wiggly worms down the backs of their shirts so they would wake up screaming.

"ARGH!"

"HO! HO! HO! HORNSWOGGLER!"

Mrs Curdle would sneeze over the orphans…

"HACHOOOO!"

…and blow her nose on their hair.

"HOOMPH! GONGOOZLER!"

A weekly "bath" involved her dunking the orphans one by one into a barrel full of maggots. "The maggots will nibble off the dirt, you muck snipes!" Mrs Curdle would snigger.

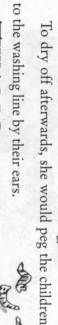

To dry off afterwards, she would peg the children to the washing line by their ears.

TWANG!

Once, when Elsie was found with a pet rat in her pocket that she had befriended, Mrs Curdle used it as a ball in a game of cricket.

THUD!

"EEEEEK!"

WHIZZ!

"HOWZAT!"

If she felt one of the orphans had given her a funny look, Mrs Curdle would poke them in the eye with her dirty, stubby finger.

"OUCH!"

"TAKE THAT, GIBFACE!"

As a special treat at Christmas, the orphans would line up for their present, a whack on the bottom with The Bumper Book of Carols.

BASH!

"Merry Christmas, child!" Mrs Curdle would exclaim with glee on each strike.

◆

Elsie endured ten long, hard years at WORMLY HALL. The only thing that kept her going was the dream that one day her ma would magically appear and whisk her away. But she never did. As the girl grew up, she would invent more and more incredible stories about her.

Perhaps her ma was a jungle explorer?

Or an acrobat with a travelling circus?

Even better, a lady pirate off having adventures on the high seas?

Every night, Elsie would make up bedtime stories for her fellow orphans. Over time, the girl became a magnificent storyteller. She had all the other children in the palm of her grubby little hand.

"Then Ma found herself in a dark, dark place. It was the belly of a huge blue whale..."

"Ma escaped from the tribe of cannibals, which wasn't easy as they had already gobbled up her left leg..."

"Boom! Ma had thrown the bomb into the Thames just in time, so no one was killed. It was all in a day's work for a secret agent. The end."

When that night's story finished, the other orphans would cry out...

"Another!"

"We don't want to go to sleep yet!"

"PLEASE, ELSIE, JUST ONE MORE!"

One night, the children cheered so much at Elsie's story that they woke up Mrs Curdle.

"NO! MORE! STORIES! YOU! NASTY! LITTLE! BEAST!"

raged the woman, beating Elsie with a broomstick on every word. The pus-sodden stocking she stuffed in the girl's mouth only half muffled her screams.

"ARGH! ARGH! ARGH!"

The beating was so severe that Elsie wasn't sure she was going to survive. Her little body was black and blue with bruises, and the girl knew she had to escape or *die*.

Chapter 2

MONKEY FEET

Elsie loved all the rats and pigeons that would find their way inside WORMLY HALL. If she had any food, she would share it with them, and tend to any broken wings and legs. In return, they would snuggle up to her, which made her feel less lonely. In her heart, Elsie felt a deep connection to these animals that Mrs Curdle called "vermin". To her, they were little creatures all alone in the world just like her.

Elsie had noticed how the rats got into the orphanage by scuttling along a leaky pipe that came down from the ceiling.

One thing that set Elsie apart from her fellow orphans was her feet. Elsie didn't have ordinary feet. She had monkey feet.

The advantage of having long, thick toes that could grip like fingers was that it made climbing easy-peasy. So one night, when everyone else was asleep, Elsie scaled the pipe to see where the rats scrambled in. Just as she had thought, there was a small rat-sized hole at the top of the wall.

After that, every night after candles out, Elsie scaled the pipe, using her monkey feet. Once at the top, she would scrape away at the brickwork with her fingernails. Night after night she scraped and scraped, making the hole bigger and bigger.

SCRATCH! SCRATCH! SCRATCH!

Eventually, the hole was just large enough for Elsie to squeeze her tiny, underfed body through it. However, she couldn't leave WORMLY HALL without saying goodbye to her twenty-five friends.

"Wake up!" she called softly. Little eyes began to appear out of the dark. "I'm going to run away tonight. Who's coming with me?"

SILENCE.

"I said, 'Who's coming with me?'"

There were murmurs of, *"I'm too scared,"* and *"Curdle'll kill us,"* and, *"They'll catch us and beat us to death."*

The littlest little'un of the lot was named Nancy. She looked up to Elsie like she was a big sister. Nancy whispered, "Where are you going?"

"I don't know," replied the girl. "Anywhere but here."

"Please don't forget about us."

"Never!"

"Promise?"

"I promise," said Elsie. "I'll see you all again one day – I know it."

"I'm going to miss your stories," said another orphan, Felix.

"Me too," added Percival.

"Next time I see you I'll tell you the **greatest** story of all."

"Good luck, Elsie," said Nancy.

"You'll always be in 'ere," replied Elsie, patting her chest.

The girl gave one last shimmy up the pipe with her monkey feet. She squeezed herself through the hole in the wall, and with one final wiggle she was gone.

PONG

Elsie ran and ran and ran, as fast as she possibly could. She didn't dare look back. She was free but alone, and now she had to fend for herself on the streets of London, even though she'd never been outside the orphanage before. The big city was a scary place, especially for a little girl. DANGER lurked in every corner.

Soon enough, though, Elsie taught herself how to steal food from the market stalls. As for a bed, she found an old tin bath to sleep in, and used old newspapers as sheets. In her mind, Elsie pretended that it was a grand four-poster bed fit for a queen.

With no home or family, Elsie was what was known as an "urchin". Victorian London was teeming with them.

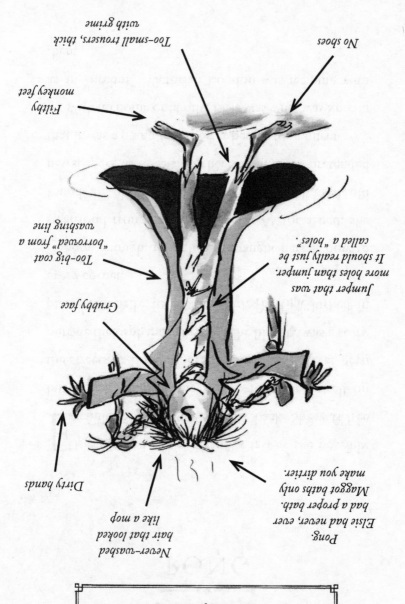

ELSIE THE URCHIN

No shoes

Too-small trousers, thick with grime

Filthy monkey feet

Too-big coat "borrowed" from a washing line

Jumper that was more holes than jumper. It should really just be called a "holes".

Grubby face

Dirty hands

Never-washed hair that looked like a mop

Pong. Elsie had never, ever had a proper bath. Maggot baths only make you dirtier.

Elsie didn't look much like a **hero**.

However, as you will soon discover,

heroes come in all

SHaPeS

and SiZeS.

Chapter 4

EXPERT THIEF

"READ ALL ABOUT IT! ICE MONSTER FOUND IN ARCTIC!"

L iving on the streets of London had its advantages. You slept under the stars. You ate all the fresh fruit and vegetables you could swipe. Best of all, you were the first to know about everything. News spread fast, and this was BIG news.

Having never been to school, Elsie couldn't read or write. However, the newspaper sellers would holler the headlines to passers-by.

The Ice Monster

Could this be true?

A real-life monster?

Ten thousand years old too?

Elsie was old enough to know that monsters weren't real, and young enough to believe that they might just be.

The girl had just swiped an apple off a market stall for her breakfast. Munching contentedly, she wove her way through the march of top-hatted gentlemen

heading for work, until she reached the newspaper stand.

"Get lost, you little thief!" shouted the newspaper seller. He whacked the girl on the back of her head with a rolled-up copy of *The Times*.

THWACK!

Chapter 5

UNIVERSE of WONDER

As an urchin, Elsie was always on the outside looking in. Every day, she would see a whole other London whirling around her.
Horse-drawn carriages
speeding down the street,

children in uniform
marching off to school,

lords and ladies stepping over
her as they left the Royal
Opera House.

Elsie's brain was forever buzzing with questions.

Where was everyone going to at such a pace?

What did those scrumptious-looking cakes in the

bakery window actually taste like?

And what was inside all those magnificent buildings?

One day, the girl decided to step out of her world and into the other.

Elsie was standing in front of the most magnificent building of all, the NATURAL HISTORY MUSEUM.

When she tried to walk in, she was immediately thrown out by the hobnail-booted brute of a security guard, Mr Clout.

"I don't want no trouble from filthy beggars like you," he shouted as he hurled her down the steps.

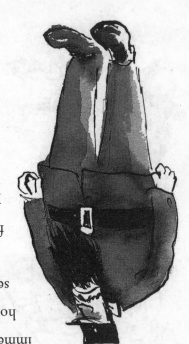

Elsie was not one to give up that easily, so she sneaked in behind a gaggle of top-hatted gentlemen.

At once, the girl marvelled at this
UNIVERSE OF **WONDER.**

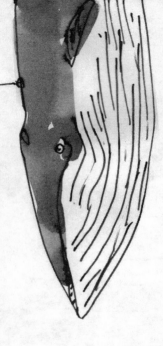

The museum was a treasure trove of life-sized models of whales…

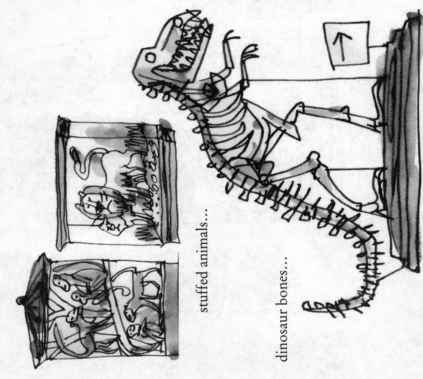

stuffed animals…

dinosaur bones…

and floor-to-ceiling paintings of creatures that had long since become extinct.

wood carvings of prehistoric men...

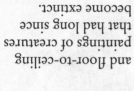

dusty old books full of beautiful pictures of animals from far-off lands...

precious stones...

meteorites...

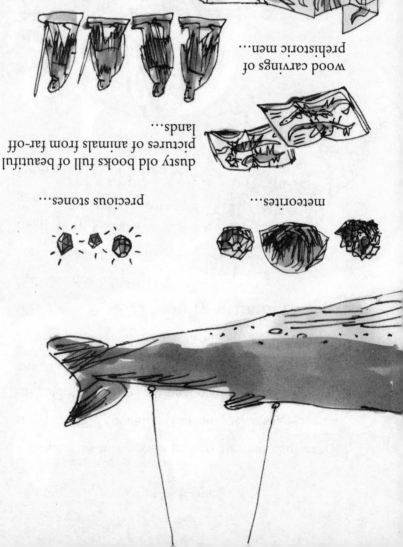

Soon she was sneaking into the museum every single day. Elsie couldn't read, but she earwigged in on the guides and soon became something of an expert. So, when she saw a picture of the **"ICE MONSTER"** on the front page of the newspaper, she knew instantly that it was, in fact, a woolly mammoth. Elsie had learned that these creatures had lived during the ICE AGE, when sabre-toothed tigers, GIANT bears,

sloths

and beavers stalked the Earth,

and birds like the *Teratornis,* a bird bigger than a person, darkened the skies.

Elsie was desperate to follow the story of the **ICE MONSTER**. So every morning she swiped another newspaper to search for news of the creature. Weeks passed, and then one day she spotted a jumble of letters she recognised on the front page of a newspaper.

They looked exactly like the ones she'd seen on the side of her favourite building.

Elsie knew she had to meet it.

•→✳←•

Chapter 6

GIANT GHOSTS

Soon after the **ICE MONSTER** was found, London was plunged into the cruellest of winters. A bitter wind brought a flurry of snow. Before long, the entire city was hushed by a thick covering of white. The River Thames froze over.

In this kind of weather, homeless children like Elsie perished in doorways. They would go to sleep and never wake up, to be found at dawn with a dusting of frost on their faces.

Poor Elsie was HUDDLING in her tin bath under a pile of newspapers, trying to keep warm.

She looked at her hands. They were shaking with the cold, and turning blue. The girl almost missed **WORMLY HALL.** Almost, but not quite.

Elsie sneaked into the **NATURAL HISTORY MUSEUM** at closing time, behind a troupe of nuns so the security guard wouldn't see her. Once inside, she scuttled along the long corridors, past the dinosaur bones hanging on wires that looked like giant ghosts, and eventually found an unlocked cupboard. She crept inside, and closed the door. It was a cleaning cupboard and too small in which to sleep lying down, so she slept standing up, with her head nestled between some mops. She looked not unlike a mop, as skinny as a rake with a shock of tangled hair on top.

Elsie was sure no one would find her in there. But she was wrong.

Very early the next morning, before dawn, Elsie was woken by a cleaning lady opening the cupboard door. The woman yawned and grabbed the first "mop" she could find. It was actually Elsie.

"AaaHHh!" screamed the lady.

"ARGH!" screamed the girl.

Elsie was being held by the neck.

"You're not a mop!" said the lady.

"No. I'm a girl."

"What are you doing in my cleaning cupboard?"

"I was sleeping. I didn't want to *die* of the cold."

"No, you don't want to do that."

Elsie gulped. "Are you going to tell on me, missus?"

The cleaning lady did the last thing the girl was expecting.

She smiled.

Most of the time, grown-ups treated urchins like Elsie with cruelty. Not this lady. She was different.

"No! *You're* not going to tell on *me*, are you?" asked the lady.

"Tell on you?" replied the girl. Elsie was befuddled. "I could lose me job over this."

"No, no, no. N**ever**. I'm not a snitch."

"Thank goodness for that. Me neither. What's your name?"

"Elsie."

"I'm Dotty. Dotty by name and, I'm told, dotty by nature. Are you a child?"

The girl was confused. She thought that was obvious. "Yes."

"I only ask because you are taller than me gentleman friend."

"How tall is he?"

"Titch is shorter than you. That isn't his real name. That's the name all the other soldiers gave him."

"How old is he?"

"Seventy-three."

"Has he shrunk?"

"Nope, God made him that way."

Dotty pulled out a dog-eared photograph from her pocket. "Here's Titch."

Elsie looked at the picture. It must have been taken a while ago, as it showed a young soldier in uniform holding a gun that was taller than him.

"He is small," remarked the girl.

"He's bigger in real life than in the photograph."

"I guessed that," replied Elsie.

"He's my hero!" said Dotty as she kissed the picture, before putting it back in her pocket. "So, I bet you're hungry."

The girl nodded her head. "Ravenous!"

Elsie was always so hungry her tummy hurt. Dotty reached into another pocket.

"Here, have me packed lunch. Bread and dripping."*

Smiling, Elsie took the food. She tore a crust of bread into halves, and handed a piece back to the lady. Both were touched by the kindness of the other.

Elsie devoured her half greedily. It was only bread and dripping, but to her it was the nectar of the gods.

"Where's your mum and dad, little one?"

"Dunno. Never met them."

"Orphan, then, are you?"

"Suppose so."

"Poor thing."

* *Dripping is fat from cooked meat.*

"There's no point feeling sorry for meself. I gotta get on with it."

At that moment, they both heard bootsteps *CLOMPING* down the corridor.

CLICK CLACK CLICK CLICK CLACK!

The lady lifted her finger to her lips to mime *"Don't say a word"* and hurriedly shut the door.

Chapter 7

A LIKELY STORY

Elsie stayed as still and quiet as she possibly could in the cleaning cupboard. Through the door, she could hear the grown-ups arguing.

"WHO ARE YOU TALKING TO, DOTTY?" boomed a voice.

"Just me mops and brushes, Mr Clout, sir," replied Dotty.

"A likely story, Dotty!" the man scoffed. "As the museum's head of security, I order you to open that door!"

"I can't."

"What do you mean, you can't?"

"Me hands have gone all floppy."

"What do you mean your hands 'have gone all floppy'?"

"Too much mopping!"

"Well, I'll open it, then."

"I wouldn't if I was you."

"Why?"

"I just *BLEW OFF* in there."

"You did what?"

"I did a bottom burp in the cupboard so all the stuffed animals wouldn't have to smell it. It's a really stinky one. It would have peeled the paint off the walls."

"That doesn't explain why you were talking."

"I was talking to my own bottom."

"You were talking to your bottom?"

"Giving it a jolly good telling-off, Mr Clout, sir."

Elsie had to put her hand over her mouth to stop herself from laughing. This lady really was dotty.

"I have never heard so much nonsense in all my life!" thundered Clout. "Now step aside, woman, or I will be forced to use… force!"

The girl heard a slight scuffle.

"*OOF!*"

"***OUCH!***"

"GET OFF ME FOOT!"

As fast as she could, Elsie nestled herself in behind the mops and brushes.

The door swung open…

Chapter 8

❖

THE UNNATURAL HISTORY MUSEUM

Clout peered inside the dark and dingy cleaning cupboard. His hulking frame all but filled up the doorway. He had huge hobnailed boots on his feet, so polished you could eat your dinner off them. The man covered his nose.

"It don't half *REEK* in here!"

That was Elsie's pong.

"Tell it to my bottom," replied Dotty.

Just then, something caught the man's eye among the mops and brushes.

"What's this?" he said, pointing at the girl's hair poking out.

"That?" asked Dotty innocently.

"Yes, that."

"Oh, that! That is one of my new real-hair mops."

"Real-hair mops?" asked Clout.

"Yes. It's great for those areas me everyday mops can't reach. Like between the dinosaurs' toe bones."

The Unnatural History Museum

"I don't think I can bear that *STINK* a moment longer," said the man, his eyes watering.

"I did warn you, Mr Clout, sir. Me blow-offs are really something."

"They should have their own museum," mused Clout. "THE UNNATURAL HISTORY MUSEUM."

"Very good, Mr Clout, sir," she said as she slammed the door shut. "It's always lovely talking to you, but, if you will excuse me, I need to give the dodo eggs a good spit and polish."

"Dotty?"

"Yes?"

"You need to get something for that bottom of yours."

"I'll invest in a cork."

"Then we'll all have to wear tin helmets in case you POP."

"That's a good point, Mr Clout. I'll try and think of something."

"Get to work!"

"You get to work!"

"I can't get to work until you get to work."

"Well, you tellin' me to get to work is stopping me from getting to work."

"GET TO WORK!" thundered the man.

Dotty picked up her mop, and began cleaning the floor. On purpose, she ran the dirty mop over his highly polished hobnailed boots.

"Me boots!" he cried.

"OOPS! Sorry!"

"Stupid old hag!"

"Less of the 'old', please, Mr Clout."

"I need to get these boots sparkling for the visitors."

"Yes, that's why they all come to the **NATURAL HISTORY MUSEUM**, Mr Clout, sir. They don't come to see the dinosaur bones. They just want to see their own face reflected in your boots. You better buff 'em up, good and proper."

Clout gave the cleaning lady a filthy look before

marching off down the corridor to make someone else's life a **misery.**

CLICK CLACK CLICK CLACK CLICK CLACK!

After a few moments, Dotty opened the cupboard door.

"*PHEW!*" said Elsie. "That was close."

"If I know Clout, he'll be back."

"I'd better get out of here."

"Are you sure you'll be all right?"

"Don't worry. I'll find somewhere else to hide tonight."

"If you're sure?"

"I'm sure."

"Folk will be trickling in soon. Now would be a good time to make a swift exit."

"I gotta ask you something."

"Yes, dearie?"

"Why have you been so kind to me?" asked Elsie.

"Why not?" came the simple answer.

The pair shared a smile before the girl shuffled off down the long corridor.

"Take care, little one," called out the cleaning lady after her. "And please come back and see me very soon."

"I will," replied Elsie.

And she did.

Chapter 9

THE DEVIL'S WORK

Every morning, Elsie checked the newspapers for more news of the **ICE MONSTER**. Weeks passed until one day she heard the cloth-capped sellers shouting from their stands...

"ICE MONSTER
TO SAIL DOWN THE THAMES!"

"ICE MONSTER
EXPECTED IN LONDON TODAY!"

"ICE MONSTER
TO BE KEPT FROZEN IN ICE
IN MUSEUM!"

The girl's heart pounded with excitement.

Up in the Arctic, the mammoth and the **huge** slab of ice in which it had been found had been packed into a wooden crate full of snow and loaded on to a whaling ship. It was then transported thousands of miles from the Arctic all the way down to the mouth of the Thames.

From there it travelled upriver towards London and its ultimate destination, the **NATURAL HISTORY MUSEUM**. The whaling ship was escorted along the Thames by a formation of gleaming new boats of the British naval fleet, which broke up the ice to allow it safe passage.

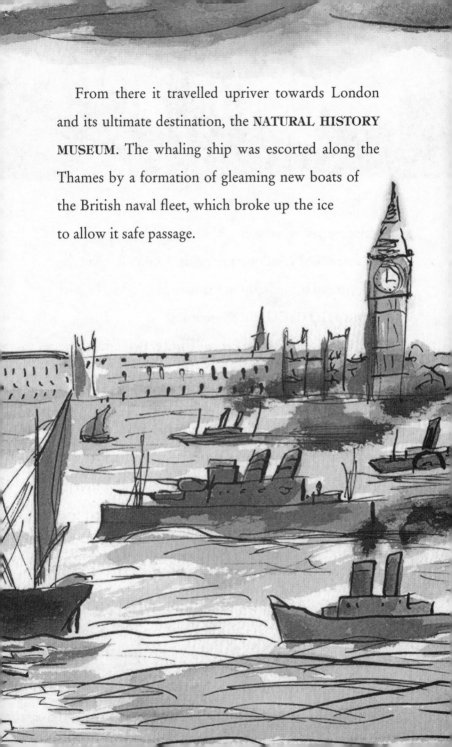

The **ICE MONSTER** was being given a huge welcome as if it were a visiting king or queen. Thousands of Londoners lined the banks all along the river to catch a glimpse of the creature, and to be part of this **momentous** occasion.

Being little, Elsie was able to crawl under the grown-ups' legs to scramble right to the front. There she could see the whaling ship, and the huge coffin-like crate into which the animal was packed.

When the ships had passed, Elsie raced across London towards the museum. Living on the streets, the girl knew every nook and cranny of the city. She *DASHED* along back streets, across gardens, down tunnels, over rooftops and even jumped on to the back

of horse-drawn cabs to get there before the monster.

A line of policemen with linked arms formed a wall round the museum as Londoners surged forward to see the wooden box trundle by on a carriage pulled by fifty mighty horses.

"HURRAH!" cheered the crowds.

But one lone voice was shouting something different. It was an old man with a long beard, wearing a big sandwich board over his shoulders. The words "THE END IS NIGH" were emblazoned across it. He held aloft a copy of the Bible, and cried, "This is the Devil's work. The prophecy has come true. The beast has come! The end is nigh!"

Elsie tugged on his coat. "It's not a **beast**, sir – it's a woolly mammoth."

The old man gave her a whack on the head with his Bible.

T*HWACK!*

"Wicked child!"

Elsie pushed past him, helping herself to a lump of mouldy cheese from his pocket as she did so. The girl had just reached the gates of the museum when she was shoved back by a policeman.

"Get back, you revolting urchin!" he bawled, and he shunted her aside.

"OUCH!" she cried as she tumbled on to her back.

"We don't want your sort here. Now clear off!"

As the lowest of the low, Elsie was used to being turned away, but, being strong in spirit, she was not going to take no for an answer. So she scrambled her way up the back of a gentleman's coat, and trod on his top hat.

SQUISH!

Before he had a chance to cry out, she leaped off his top hat and on to the branch of a nearby tree.

TWANG!

With her monkey feet, Elsie shimmied up the tree with ease, and stood on the highest branch. From there, she watched as a hundred men rolled the crate off the back of the carriage. With thick ropes, they heaved it up the stone steps.

The huge wooden front doors of the museum had been taken off their hinges. The crowd fell silent as the men began pushing the crate through the doorway. Would it fit in without taking the front of the NATURAL HISTORY MUSEUM with it?

A cheer went up as the crate just squeezed through.

"HURRAH!"

Soon mutterings passed around the crowd that a very important visitor would be coming to the museum today to witness the unveiling.

"She's coming here?"

"Who?"

"You know!"

"Oh, my Lord!"

"Not her?"

"Yes, her!"

"She ain't been seen in ages."

"She's so old now."

"This must really be something."

"I should have bought a new hat!"

Sure enough, barely an hour had passed before the streets echoed with the sound of trumpets.

Bruh duh duh duh duh duh duh

All heads turned to see a golden carriage trundling along the road. Ahead of the carriage, liveried soldiers on horseback blew trumpets to herald the arrival of the very important person seated in it.

Queen Victoria.

Chapter 10

HULLABALOO

This was a day that would go down in history, so it was only fitting that the most powerful person in the world should be there. 'Queen Victoria was not just the Queen of Great Britain and Ireland, but the monarch of a vast empire that spanned the globe. She had even adopted the title of "Empress of India", despite the fact that she'd never actually been there.

These were different days.

As the crowd realised that they were in the presence of their queen, a woman who'd reigned over them for more than sixty years, they erupted in wild cheers, throwing their hats into the air.

"HURRAH!"

The golden carriage turned to the right to pass through the gates of the museum, and Elsie seized her chance. While the sky was black with hats, she leaped off the branch of the tree...

WHOOSH!

...and landed on top of the Queen's carriage.

THUD!

With all the noise and commotion, no one seemed to notice this huge breach of security.

Elsie lay down flat on the roof of the carriage so she wouldn't be seen. In 1899, anyone getting this close

to Her Majesty without an invitation might very well pay the price with their life.

The carriage sped into the grounds of the museum, and came to a halt at the bottom of the stone steps. Elsie lifted her head a tiny bit, and peeked over the side of the carriage.

Thousands of faces were pushed up against the metal railings, open mouths roaring their approval for their queen.

"HURRAH!"

The carriage wobbled slightly as Her Majesty stepped out. The Queen was old and frail, and tottered up the stone steps, helped by a handsome Indian attendant in a turban. She was dressed from head to toe in black and wore a solemn look on her face.

That was because she was in deep mourning for her husband, Prince Albert, even though he had died nearly forty years before. Not wanting to disappoint the crowd, the Queen slowly turned round and gave them a polite wave.

"HURRAH!"

While all eyes were on the royal guest, Elsie slid off the roof and lowered herself down the side of the carriage. There she hid behind a wheel.

The hullabaloo must have startled the horses…

"NEIGH! NEIGH!"

…as the carriage shunted backwards a little. Elsie thought she was going to be trampled to death by the horses' hooves, but the carriage driver cracked his whip…

SNAP!

…and ordered…

"WHOA!"

Elsie let out a sigh of relief as the horses came to a juddering stop.

The girl watched from her hiding place as the

Queen was greeted with a bow by the director of the museum, the portly Sir Ray Lankester, and led inside. The huge wooden doors were closed behind her.

THUD.

Now Elsie wasn't feeling too clever. All around her she could see the legs of policemen. How was she going to get inside that museum without anyone seeing her? She was desperate to do so, but Elsie had more chance of becoming the next Archbishop of Canterbury.

As she pondered her next move on her hands and knees, the most unexpected thing happened. The carriage moved off, leaving the girl hiding behind nothing at all. She was concealed only by some air.

Air is the worst thing to find yourself hiding behind. Other bad ones include:

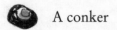 A conker

A marble

A wasp   A rabbit dropping

A pea

A flea   A speck of dust

An amoeba

An amoeba dropping

The invisible man

Elsie was in deep, deep doo-doo.

·→✳←·

Chapter 11

❖

HUMAN NET

"HA! HA!" the crowd outside the **NATURAL HISTORY MUSEUM** all laughed when the little urchin was revealed hiding behind the air.

The policemen looked around in confusion.

"THERE!"

The crowd pointed at the girl, and eventually the policemen saw what was right under their noses.

They formed a circle round this uninvited guest, and began closing in on her.

Having lived on the streets, Elsie was no stranger to running away from the police, or the "rozzers"* as those who spent most of their time running away from the police called them.

The policemen crouched down and stretched out their arms, sure that she would try to escape by running through their legs.

"We've got you!" growled the chief of police, Commissioner Barker. He was a heavy man with a tiny postage stamp of a moustache stuck over his top lip.

The circle was closing.

The policemen linked arms to make themselves into a human net.

There was no way out.

Spotting the truncheons dangling from their belts, a daring thought crossed Elsie's mind. Just as the policemen were looming over her, she grabbed two of the truncheons with each hand, yanking them as hard as she could.

---

* *"Rozzers" is a slang term for the police, loosely echoing the first name of their founder, Robert Peel.*

This brought the policemen crashing towards one another.

Their heads knocked together.

BISH! BASH! BOSH!

"OW!"

"OOF!"

"ARGH!"

Dazed and confused, the policemen tumbled backwards, and collapsed on to the ground.

From above, the scene looked like a flower, with Elsie the centre and the policemen all splayed-out petals.

This brilliant move by the urchin instantly won over the crowd, and they cheered.

"HURRAH!"

No one wanted to see an army of policemen win against one little mite.

However, there was no time to lap up the attention of the crowd. Elsie darted up the steps towards the entrance to the NATURAL HISTORY MUSEUM. Another squad of policemen stood guard in front of the huge wooden doors. They drew their truncheons, ready to give this little creature a ruddy good bashing.

Not wanting to receive a bashing, be it a good or a bad one (neither sounded appealing), Elsie slid down the handrail. To one side of the building entrance was a drainpipe.

There was no time to think. What with her monkey feet, Elsie was soon halfway up it.

"HURRAH!" cheered the crowd once more. One bold policeman gave chase up the drainpipe, but not being blessed with monkey feet he instantly slid back down.

WHIZZ!

"ARGH!"

His bottom landed right on top of another policeman's face.

BOING!

"POOH!" complained the one whose nose was now stuck up the other's rear end.

Needless to say, this perfect piece of slapstick was greeted by howls of laughter from the crowd.

"HA! HA! HA!"

"AFTER HER, YOU FOOLS!"

barked Barker.

"Right away, Commissioner, sir!" said one.

"FORM A LADDER!" ordered the commissioner.

"How are we gonna do that?"

"Heaviest at the bottom."

"That's very kind of you, sir."

Barker fumed. His tiny moustache twitched. "I am not part of the ladder! I am in charge! Now, the heaviest at the bottom, then the next heaviest, then the next, and so on and so forth."

The policemen all started arguing among themselves. No one wanted to be at the bottom.

"I'm the lightest!"

"No. I'm the lightest!"

"You're the heaviest by far!"

"I've lost weight."

"You still look fat."

"I've just got a round face."

"SHE'S GETTING AWAY!"

thundered Barker.

The girl was nearing the top of the drainpipe. The commissioner took charge of his human ladder, quickly ordering who went where. Soon the policemen were reluctantly climbing on top of one another.

Needless to say, this amateur acrobatics act immediately came crashing to the ground.

"OOF!"

"OUCH!"

"ARGH!"

"EEK!"

"HELP! Someone's trodden on me bits!"

The crowd whooped and cheered at this brilliant piece of entertainment.

"HURRAH!"

By this time, Elsie had reached the roof of the museum. She took a moment to acknowledge her adoring audience, and gave them a little bow.

The crowd burst into wild applause.

"YES!"

"SHE'S DONE IT!"

"GO! GO! GO!"

The little girl hurried over the sloping roofs to the far side of the building, her **monkey feet** gripping the lead. For a moment, looking over the rooftops of London, she felt immortal. However, when a tile slipped from under her, she suddenly felt distinctly mortal.

The tile exploded on to the ground.

Instantly, Elsie slammed down on to the roof…

THUD!

…and began sliding down it at speed.

"AAAH!"

The girl rolled over in a desperate attempt to grab

on to the roof. Just as she was about to fly off, she managed to hook her fingers round the guttering.

However, Elsie was going so fast she swung forward. Her fingers unhooked and she felt herself hurtling through the air.

"NOOO!"

Chapter 12

SABRE-TOOTHED TEETH

Elsie flew forward and burst through a stained-glass window.

SHATTER!

She rolled down some stone steps before landing on top of a glass cabinet that housed the skeleton of a sabre-toothed tiger.

THUD!

Elsie came down with such force that the sheet of glass on which she landed began to crack.

KERCHUNK!

Like a shaft of lightning splintering through the sky, the crack shot across the glass.

BING!

In a split second, the glass panel at the top of the cabinet misted over as it became a thousand tiny pieces.

Elsie knew exactly what was going to happen next, but was powerless to stop it. She gulped. The glass crumbled beneath her, and Elsie fell into the cabinet, landing on the back of the sabre-toothed tiger.

CRUNCH!   "*OOF!*"

Now the girl was trapped inside the glass cabinet, and with all the noise from the window smashing she was sure to have drawn attention to herself. If only there were some way of breaking one of the glass walls, but they were inches thick. However hard she thumped with her fists, it just wouldn't break.

BOOM! BOOM! BOOM!

Feeling that there was little chance of the sabre-toothed tiger skeleton missing it, she pulled out one of its sabre-toothed teeth. With an almighty swing of her arm, she bashed the sharp end of the tooth against the glass.

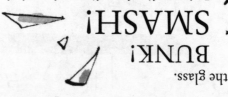

BUNK! SMASH!

It immediately splintered, and the tiny pieces of glass showered down like rain.

PATTER!

Not needing the tooth any more, Elsie stuck it back where she'd found it, and patted the sabre-toothed tiger skeleton in thanks.

"Good boy!"

The sound of bootsteps echoed along the corridor.

CLICK CLACK CLICK CLACK CLICK CLACK!

It must be the museum's head of security, Mr Clout. Elsie knew she had to make a run for it. Having no shoes on her feet, she carefully stepped over the pieces of broken glass, and charged off down a corridor. Staying close to the walls and keeping out of the light – something she had learned from the rats at the orphanage – she found a balcony overlooking the main hall.

From the top floor of the museum, Elsie looked down on the **historic scene.**

Chapter 13

A SEA OF OLD MEN

◆

Sitting on a grand chair that made her look even smaller than her actual size (and she already looked extremely small) was ᚺQueen Victoria.

Gathered behind her was a sea of old men with white beards, spectacles and stern expressions. They looked like learned men: scientists, explorers and politicians.

Mr Clout circled the room like a hungry shark, ready to attack anyone who made a lunge for Her Majesty. Commisioner Barker was doing the exact same thing. The pair kept on bumping into each other.

"OOF!"

"OUT OF THE WAY, YOU FOOL!"

growled Barker.

Masked by a red velvet curtain, something the size of a house was standing in front of the tiny queen.

A portly man stepped forward and addressed the gathering. He was the director of the **NATURAL HISTORY MUSEUM**, Sir Ray Lankester.

"Your Majesty, my lords, gentlemen..." he began.

"SPEAK UP!" shouted Queen Victoria.

Elsie put her hand over her mouth to stifle a giggle. She wouldn't have had Her Majesty down as a heckler.

Poor Lankester looked aghast, as you might if the most powerful person in the world was barracking you. The man tried to carry on as best he could.

"YOUR MAJESTY, MY LORDS, LADIES AND GENTLEMEN," he began again, his voice cracking with nerves. "As director of the

NATURAL HISTORY MUSEUM, it is a huge honour to house what I am sure you will all agree is the greatest find of the century. When a group of explorers set off across the Arctic…"

"GET ON WITH IT!" shouted the Queen.

"Yes, yes, of course, Your Majesty. I am very sorry. I know you have an empire to run. Will you please do us all the honour of unveiling this creature dubbed the 'ICE MONSTER', which has been perfectly preserved in the ice for thousands of years?"

With some difficulty, the Queen stood up. Her handsome attendant Abdul Karim went to help her.

"I can do it, thank you very much, Munshi!"* she snapped.

"As you wish, Your Majesty," he purred.

"Actually, can you help me?" she asked, looking a little wobbly.

Abdul gracefully took her arm, and she shuffled over to the exhibit.

"It gives one great pleasure," began the Queen, "to declare this woolly mammoth open."

---

* "Munshi" was the fond title Queen Victoria gave Abdul. It is a Persian word which means "secretary", though he was a great deal more than that to her.

With that, she tugged on the cord, and the velvet
curtain slipped to the floor.

S I L E N C E .

There it was.

In all its glory.

Housed in a huge glass tank.

Suspended in ice.

The mammoth.

Perfectly preserved.

A Sea of Old Men

It was impossible to believe it had been dead for ten thousand years. To all appearances, it could have died yesterday.

The creature looked like a cross between an elephant and a teddy bear. The tusks were **long** and curled, like the moustaches of many of the fusty old men gathered in the museum. Between the tusks hung a long, furry trunk. The mammoth's body was covered in coarse brown hair, with a thicker and darker tuft on its head like a wig. Its legs were as wide as tree trunks, leading down to four clumpy feet. Its eyes were open. They were small and black, and shaped like tears.

For Elsie, it was **love** at first sight.

This was the most beautiful thing she had ever seen. Her heart soared, and her mind began dancing with pictures.

Here she was stroking the animal's fur. There she was riding on its back. Then she was being held by its long, furry trunk.

Just as she was flying off into a land of make-believe, Elsie sensed someone standing right behind her. The girl was frozen in fear. She couldn't even turn her head to look round. Then she felt a hand come to rest on her shoulder. Elsie gasped for air to let out a cry…

"HUH!"

…but she couldn't.

A hand was covering her mouth.

. ⇀ ✳ ↽ .

Chapter 14

DEAD as DEAD CAN BE

"S**hush!**" came the voice behind her. "Don't give yourself away."

Elsie knew that voice. It was the only adult voice she ever remembered speaking to her in a tone of kindness.

DOTTY'S.

Elsie turned round and whispered, "Thank goodness it's you."

"Everyone, but everyone, is looking for you, young miss."

"I know. I'm not supposed to be here."

"You don't say!" replied the cleaning lady. "Truth

be told, I'm not supposed to be here either. A humble cleaner isn't allowed to be in the same room as Her Queen the Majesty."

"Her Majesty the Queen?"

Dotty looked at the girl as if she were bonkers. "That's what I said. But I couldn't resist being here. I love our Queen." Dotty gazed down proudly at the lady. "Ooh, that reminds me. I must buy a stamp."

Two stories below, the Queen was looking up at the frozen creature.

"Well, well, well. So this is the famous '**ICE MONSTER**'?"

"Yes, ma'am," replied the director. "It is a huge feat of engineering for the museum to keep the animal's body conserved like this. That pipe you can see hanging down from the ceiling blows cold air into the tank through that hatch to keep the ice it is packed in frozen."

"It's a bit small for a monster."

Lankester was once again blindsided by the lady.

"Well, I, er, um," he spluttered. "I can only

apologise, Your Majesty, but this mammoth is probably only a year or so old. It's a child, really."

The Queen looked lost in thought for a moment. "Have you got any **bigger** ones?"

Lankester looked desperately around at the faces of the assembled great and good for help, but none came.

"Er, um, no. I am afraid not, ma'am. Finding any prehistoric creature, let alone one in such perfect condition, is **extremely rare**. This is the End of the century."

"Mmm. My dear departed husband, Prince Albert, would have liked it. Such a shame he isn't here with me to see this. Albert loved animals. I am more of an opera fan myself, aren't I, Munshi?"

Her elegant companion smiled weakly. "You have a unique singing voice, Your Majesty."

His wry answer made the old lady chuckle.

"*HA! HA! HA!*"

The chuckle turned into a cough.

"Huh, huh, huh."

A concerned Abdul steadied her.

"Thank you, Munshi. I don't know what I would do without you."

"Nor me without you, Your Majesty."

The unlikely pair shared a smile, then the Queen looked back up at the mammoth.

"Does it do anything?" she enquired.

"I am so sorry, Your Majesty, what do you mean?" replied Lankester. Sweat was now pouring off his brow.

"Like a trick?" she asked with girlish excitement.

The museum's director paused before he spoke, gathering his thoughts. "Sadly not, Your Majesty.

This creature has been dead for ten thousand years. So, as *DEAD* goes, I would say you can't get much *DEADER*. It's as *DEAD* as *DEAD* as *DEAD* can be."

"Oh. That is a shame. I suppose it is rather pretty, if you like that sort of thing. Which I do."

Lankester shuffled awkwardly. "Do you have any other questions, Your Majesty?"

The Queen thought for a moment. "When are we having the **tea and cake?** I was dragged halfway across London to come here. These days I don't like to leave the palace too much. At my age, it all becomes a bit of a bother. But my eyes lit up at the promise of tea and cake, you see, and I haven't seen so much as a scone."

"I meant any questions about the *MAMMOTH*, Your Majesty."

"The what?"

"This creature here."

"**No,**" replied the Queen with her customary bluntness.

Dead as Dead Can Be

"Shame it's *DEAD* already," came a deep voice from the shadows of the hall. "Or I would **shoot it.**"

All heads turned to see who had so rudely interrupted Her Majesty the Queen.

Chapter 15

EXTINCTION BUSINESS

Out of the darkness stepped a figure dressed in a pith helmet, knee-high lace-up boots and a khaki coat. A plume of grey cigar smoke followed it.

"Who the blazes is that?" demanded the Queen, struggling to see.

"Oh n-no," stammered Lankester.

"Who is it?"

"Lady Buckshot the big-game hunter, Your Majesty," replied Lankester.

"Oh no!" agreed the Queen.

Disapproving murmurs echoed around the hall.

"What is she doing here?" pressed the Queen.

"Well, ma'am," replied the hunter, "I shot and killed every single stuffed animal in the museum."

"Such a shame the animals weren't armed, or they

could have fired back," hissed the Queen to Abdul, just loud enough for Buckshot to hear.

"*HA! HA!*" Abdul couldn't help but laugh.

"It's a shame this here monster is already dead," began Buckshot. "It would have been my great pleasure to shoot it, right between the eyes."

"Well, erm, um, L-L-Lady Buckshot," spluttered Lankester, "the mammoth as a species has long since been extinct."

"I am in the extinction business," replied the hunter. "I would wipe out every last creature on Earth if I could."

"How delightful for you!" said the Queen sarcastically. "Now, where is this tea and cake?"

Lankester leaped in. "Tea and cakes will now be served in the gallery. If you would follow me…"

The Queen took Abdul's arm, and she shuffled out of the hall.

The great and the good all followed, which left Buckshot alone with the mammoth. From the top of the stairs, Elsie and Dotty watched as she marched right up to the front of the tank. There she mimed taking out a shotgun, loading it and firing. **"BOOM!"** She even provided a sound effect, before miming the mammoth's brains splurging out.

"Ha! Ha! Ha!" she chuckled to herself,

before drifting back into the shadows.

Now only Elsie and Dotty were left
in the main hall.

"I am trembling!" chattered Elsie, holding
on to the balcony rail. The evil stench of Buckshot's
cigar smoke had snaked all the way up there.

"Me too. Evil woman. She's always dragging in
some poor tiger or lion she's shot, with a wicked grin
on her face."

"So, now she's gone, do we dare?" asked the girl.

"Dare what?" replied the cleaning lady.

"Do we dare to go down and take a closer look?"

Dotty shook her head. "Ooh, Elsie, you'll get me
into deep doo-doo."

"Let's just have a very, very, VERY quick look."

When the girl put it that way, it was hard to say no.

"A very quick look?" asked Dotty.

"A glance, really."

"A glimpse?"

"Less than a glimpse, a peep."

"A peek?"

"*EXACTLY!*" replied Elsie.

Dotty sighed heavily. "All right, then. Let's have a peek at this mammoth."

"I think it's 'mammoth'," corrected Elsie.

"Yes, 'mammoth'! That's what I said."

Elsie smiled, and pulled the lady along by her sleeve. "Dotty, come on…"

Chapter 16

CHEEKS ABLAZE

"I am not sliding down the banister!" protested Dotty.

"But it's the fastest way down!" replied Elsie.

Dotty was right to be reluctant. It was an awfully long way from the topmost floor of the museum to the bottommost.

"In the time we've been arguing, we could already be at the bottom," reasoned Elsie.

The girl clambered on to the banister. Dotty sighed, then hitched up her skirt and joined her.

"This is a very extremely bad idea," said the lady.

It was too late.

WHOOSH!

"Ouch. Me bottom cheeks are ablaze!" complained Dotty.

"**HOLD ON!**" called out Elsie.

Soon they ran out of banister.

The girl landed on the floor.

THUD!

Dotty landed on top of her.

THUDDER!

Mesmerised, Elsie approached the **ICE MONSTER**. All that was separating the girl from a species that had become extinct thousands of years ago were a few inches of glass and ice.

"Funny-looking thing," muttered Dotty.

"I think it's **beautiful,**" whispered the girl. "It's like the biggest cuddly toy in the whole wide world."

Dotty chuckled. "I'm not sure it would be all that

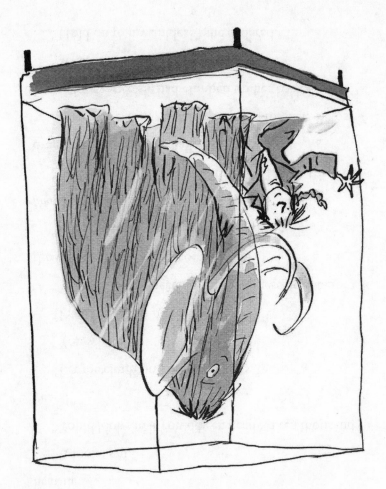

cuddly if it was alive. Now come on. We need to get
out of here before Mr Clout comes back."

The girl stood still.

"Elsie? ELSIE?"

The lady tugged at the little girl's arm. "We need to go."

"I don't want to leave it alone here," replied Elsie.

"You what?" Dotty couldn't believe what she was hearing.

"It looks sad."

"You'd look sad if you'd been dead for ten thousand years!"

"Let me climb on your shoulders."

"You what?"

"I need to take a closer look."

"Young lady, we need to get out of here now, before the Queen Her Majesty comes back."

"Quicker than a peek," implored Elsie. "A *peek-a-boo*! I promise."

"No! Now come on!" With that, Dotty tried to drag the girl out of the hall.

However, Elsie was far too quick for her. Before Dotty knew it, Elsie had climbed up her back.

"What the…?"

"Hold on to my ankles!" she ordered.

Elsie stood on the lady's shoulders as a reluctant Dotty dutifully held on to her. The girl was now at head height with the mammoth. She pressed her nose up against the cold glass, and stared deep into one of its little black eyes.

"What are you doing up there?" called Dotty.

The truth was Elsie didn't exactly know what she was doing up there. All she did know was that she was **transfixed**. She didn't move. It was as if she were frozen solid too.

"**We need to go!**" implored Dotty.

Still Elsie stared. Then the most magical thing happened. It was a moment that changed everything.

A bead of water formed in the creature's eye.

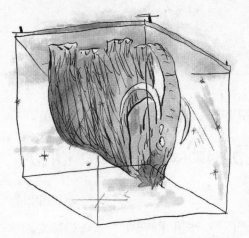

"**It's crying!**" called down Elsie.

"Oh, my! You're imagining things, young lady. That manmoth hasn't cried since long before even I was born. Now come down!"

"Not yet."

"What do you mean, 'not yet'?"

"'Not yet' means 'not yet'."

Down the corridor, there was the sound of bootsteps.

CLICK CLACK CLICK CLACK CLICK CLACK!

Clout was on to them.

"We need to go! Now!" cried Dotty. With the girl still standing on her shoulders, she began running as fast as she could.

"WHOA!" exclaimed Elsie as she tried to stop wobbling.

CLICK CLACK CLICK CLACK CLICK CLACK!

"*WHO GOES THERE?*" Clout's shout echoed along the corridor.

Elsie toppled over and slid down Dotty's back.

Now she was riding her like a horse.

"Giddy-up!" ordered the girl as together they made their escape.

Chapter 17

CURIOUS
CREATURES

I n her many years of working there, Dotty had cleaned every inch of the NATURAL HISTORY MUSEUM. She knew all the best hiding places.

"**Down here!**" hissed the lady as she led Elsie down some stone steps. Ahead of them stood a huge metal door with a sign that read:

Dotty fished in her pocket and pulled out a jangling bunch of keys.

"It's one of these," she muttered to herself.

"But which one?" pressed Elsie.

"I know it's a metal one."

"They're all metal! They're keys! Give them here."

Elsie snatched the keys off Dotty, and after a few attempts found the right one. She unlocked the door, and ushered Dotty inside. Then, as quietly as she could, the girl closed the door behind them, and locked it.

CLUNK.

Listening through the thick metal, the pair heard the sound of bootsteps descending the stairs.

CLICK CLACK CLICK CLACK CLICK CLACK!

The door handle was turned...

RATTLE.

The pair held their breath.

There followed the sound of bootsteps ascending the stairs.

CLICK CLACK CLICK CLACK CLICK CLACK...

The pair exhaled.

"Thank goodness Clout doesn't have his keys," whispered Elsie.

"No," replied Dotty. "They're right here!" she added, holding up the set in her hand. "I lost mine so I borrowed his."

"Clever Dotty!"

"I'm not just a pretty face!" said the cleaning lady. Elsie smiled. There was no answer to that. "So, where are we?"

"The NATURAL HISTORY MUSEUM in London."

"Yes, I know that, Dotty! I mean *where* in the NATURAL HISTORY MUSEUM in London?"

"Oh, we're in the storeroom. Now stay close to me…"

If upstairs was full of wonders, downstairs was even more so. The storeroom was full of things that were too weird to be put on show.

The pair passed a number of curious creatures pickled in tanks. There was a shark with two heads, a giant tortoise the size of a baby elephant and a snake

as long as a cricket pitch. Overlooking them were stuffed conjoined twin OWLS, a mighty lump of red rock that looked like it had fallen to Earth from another planet...

and an egg so big it must have belonged to a *Megalosaurus*. A prehistoric human skull squatted on a plinth. It was bizarre-looking, half human and half ape.

"What's this?" asked the girl.

Dotty ambled over. "Dunno. I wouldn't touch it if I was you. It looks spooky."

"If you think that skull looks spooky, you've never met Mrs Curdle."

"Who?"

"She ran the orphanage I escaped from. And she's got warts bigger than this!"

Elsie rested her hand on top of the skull, and it wobbled slightly. Intrigued, the girl rotated the top piece of the skull back from the jaw.

CREAK!

Suddenly, the pair realised they were spinning round!

Elsie touching the skull had opened
a secret door!
Now they were plunged
into total darkness.
"Argh!" they screamed.

WhiiiiiiiiiiiiiiiiiiiizzzzZZZZZiiiiiiii

Chapter 18

DARKEST DARK

"Something's grabbing hold of me!" yelled Dotty.

"Something's grabbing hold of me!" yelled Elsie.

"HELP!" they screamed.

"I think we might be grabbing hold of each other," said the girl.

"Oh yes."

"Shall we let go?"

"Yes."

They did so.

"That's better," said Dotty.

"Where are we?" asked Elsie.

"Still in the **NATURAL HISTORY MUSEUM** in London."

"YES! I KNOW THAT!"

"ALL RIGHT!"

"I mean, where in the museum are we?"

"Dunno!" answered Dotty. "I've been cleaning this place for donkey's years and I ain't never been in here. It must be a secret room."

"A secret room! Cor blimey!" Elsie couldn't hide her excitement. "Let's explore!"

"You go first," said Dotty, "I'll be right behind you in case of an attack from the rear."

Knowing the old dear was frightened, Elsie said, "Hold my hand."

Together they made their way across the dark room towards a faint flicker of light. On closer inspection, it turned out to be a dusty old bottle, thick with cobwebs. The girl blew on the bottle to reveal its contents. A light was dancing under the glass. It was as if a ghost were trapped in there.

"It's alive," said Elsie.

"How can a bottle be alive?"

"Dunno. But look – something's inside."

Dotty peered in. "Very queer. Whatever you do, DON'T TOUCH IT!"

Like most children, Elsie had selective hearing and, on this occasion, chose **not** to listen. She reached out her hand to touch the bottle.

"Ouch!" she yelled, recoiling in pain.

"What did I tell you?"

"It's hot!"

The girl pulled down the sleeve of her coat to save her fingers from being burned.

"I wonder what's inside?" she pondered.

"Whatever you do," repeated Dotty, "DON'T OPEN IT."

Again, the child chose not to listen, and slowly she began easing the cork out of the bottle.

"I said 'don't'!" repeated Dotty.

POP!

A bolt of light shot out, illuminating the room for a split second in brilliant bright white.

Z A N G !

"ELSIE!" shouted Dotty.

It was too late.

The fizzing beam hit Elsie, and her whole body
LIT UP.

Jolts
of light
buzzed
all over her.

"AAAHHH!" she screamed. Her hair
stood on end and smoke billowed from her ears.

Was she going to explode?

Then as quickly as the light had appeared it disappeared. Elsie slumped to the floor like a sack of potatoes. THUD...

SPLOSH!

The next thing Elsie knew was that she was wet. Soaking wet. Her eyes opened to see Dotty standing over her, holding a bucket.

SPLOSH!

Another wave of freezing-cold water drenched her.

SPLOSH!

And another!

Next the lady began slapping the girl around her face.

SLAP! SLAP! SLAP! SLAP!

"Wake up, Elsie! WAKE UP! Please! Don't die on me!"

"ALL RIGHT! ALL RIGHT! I AM AWAKE!"

she called up.

Dotty began shaking the girl just to make sure.

"STOP SHAKING ME!"

"Sorry!" said Dotty.

"What on earth was in that bottle? My reading ain't so good."

The lady read aloud what was scrawled on the label.

"*Lightning.*"

"Lightning in a bottle?"

"That's what it says."

"How can you catch lightning in a bottle? That's impossible."

"**Nothing is impossible, child,**" came a voice from the shadows.

Chapter 19

LIGHTNING IN A BOTTLE

D own in the secret room, the two intruders froze in fear as a figure wheeled himself out of the darkness, holding a lantern. The man was so elderly he had the appearance of a tortoise. He was completely bald, and wore a pair of half-moon spectacles on the end of his nose. His clothes were a dirty old laboratory coat worn over a tweed suit that was falling apart at the seams. He had gnarled slippers on his feet, and fingerless gloves on his callus-encrusted hands.

"It's you!" cried Dotty.
"Everyone thought you were dead!"

"No, lowly cleaning woman, I am very much alive!"

"Who is he?" said the girl.

"I am the professor!" he announced grandly.

"Professor of what?" asked Elsie.

"Exactly!" joked Dotty. "Everyone at the museum knew him. He used to be one of the top men here, until the—"

"Yes! Yes!" the professor interrupted. "We don't need to go into all that."

"What's all that?" asked Elsie, intrigued.

"The professor nearly burned the whole museum down in one of his madcap experiments!" said Dotty. The old man's face turned a furious shade of purple. "That is not what happened, you stupid, stupid woman!"

"Well then, what did happen, you not-quite-as-clever-as-you-think man?"

The girl couldn't help but smirk. Here were two grown-ups bickering like children.

The professor wheeled himself about his secret laboratory, lighting the candles around the space one by one.

Soon a room was revealed, the likes of which neither
Elsie nor Dotty had ever seen before.

There were glass tubes everywhere, chemicals in dusty old bottles and scientific equations scribbled in chalk on every inch of the walls. It was like being able to see inside the old man's brain.

Brilliant but bonkers.

"I was conducting a revolutionary experiment to harness the power of lightning," continued the professor. "Something I had been working on for many years. One stormy night ten years ago, I launched a small metal-tipped balloon into the sky. Attached to the balloon was a length of copper wire. The wire led down to that bottle that now lies smashed on the ground."

"So what happened?" asked Elsie, intrigued.

"I'll tell you what happened—" interrupted Dotty.

"Do you mind if I tell my own story, thank you

very much, you ignorant, ignorant woman?" asked the professor.

"I ain't got a clue what 'ignorant' means," scolded the woman. "But it better not be something bad!"

"My experiment was a complete success," continued the professor. "I captured lightning in a bottle. That is what gave you that little electric shock."

"Little?" exclaimed Elsie.

"Anything bigger and it would have killed you," replied the professor. "Sizzled to death in a heartbeat."

Elsie gulped. "So, if the experiment was a complete success, why did you lose your job?" she asked.

"Good question!" murmured Dotty.

"SILENCE!" ordered the professor. "The copper wire became wrapped round one of the museum's towers. Another much stronger bolt of lightning hit the balloon, and it set the tower on fire."

Dotty jumped in. "It's very lucky that it was raining cats and dogs that night or the fire would've burned the whole museum down to the ground."

The professor fell silent for a moment, then bowed

his head in sorrow. "I was hauled in front of the museum director and told in no uncertain terms that I was never to practise science again. I was thrown out! But the museum was my life – I had nowhere else to go – so I hid down here in the cellar."

"It was so long ago now, all us upstairs thought you were dead."

"I might as well be," murmured the old man. "Now I'm just rotting away in the dark, waiting for the end. My dream of becoming one of the world's most famous scientists is nothing but ashes. I have more chance of capturing lightning in a bottle!"

You got whacked by grown-ups every day if you were an urchin. You were the lowest of the low. At least it made a welcome change from being battered with a broomstick at 𝕎𝕆ℝ𝕄𝕃𝕐 ℍ𝔸𝕃𝕃.

"I only want to look!" pleaded Elsie.

"These papers is not for looking at. They is for buying. Now scram! Before I give you a kick where the sun don't shine!"

Not being a fan of a boot up the bottom, Elsie smiled at the man and ambled off down the street. She turned into an alleyway, then reached into the back of her grubby trousers and pulled out a copy of *The Times*. The girl had become an expert thief.

There were **big, bold black** letters on the front page. Elsie knew these spelled out words, but it all looked like a jumble to her. The picture underneath did speak to her, though. It was of a peculiar creature that looked like an elephant.

Once, she'd poked her head through the flap in a circus tent to get a free show, and seen an elephant performing tricks. However, *this* elephant was covered in thick hair, and its tusks were long and curved. It was encased in a huge block of ice, and a number of Arctic explorers were standing around it, looking proud. Despite the creature's bizarre appearance, Elsie found it hard to think of the poor thing as a monster. Monsters you were scared of. This animal you wanted to **hug.**

It looked a great deal smaller than the elephant she'd seen at the circus. Perhaps it was a baby. Despite having been dead for thousands of years, it still looked lost and alone.

"An orphan,"
whispered Elsie to herself.
"Just like me."

Elsie's face lit up. A thought had flashed across her mind. It was an idea so crazy it was brilliant, and so brilliant it was crazy. "I think there's still a chance your name could go down in history."

"How?" spluttered the old man.

"You could help bring a prehistoric creature back to life."

Chapter 20

DARK FIRE

"Not the sabre-toothed tiger!" exclaimed Dotty.

"NO!" laughed Elsie. "That's just a skeleton!"

"No. I suppose there's little help for that now. You don't mean the manmoth, do you?"

"The 'mammoth', yes."

"That's what I said," protested the lady. "Manmoth. You want to bring that manmoth upstairs back to life?"

"YES!"

"So we have a new arrival, do we?" asked the professor. "I wondered what all that noise was."

"Bringing it back to life is madness!" exclaimed Dotty.

"Good madness or bad madness?" asked Elsie.

"Is there a *good* kind?"

"YES! Listen, that creature has been perfectly

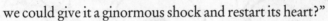

preserved for ten thousand years. It looks like it snuffed it yesterday. Right?"

Dotty nodded her head.

"So surely with the professor's lightning-catching thingummyjig we could give it a ginormous shock and restart its heart?"

Elsie and Dotty looked at the professor. He was the science expert after all, even though he had very nearly burned the **NATURAL HISTORY MUSEUM** down to the ground. His old eyes lit up with a dark fire. He stared straight ahead as the plan began to take shape in his mind.

"This is a genius idea of mine!" he whispered.

Elsie looked mightily confused. Wasn't it *her* idea?

"I can use my lightning technology to create life! The dream of all scientists since the dawn of time. To be God!"

"I think it's gone to his head a bit," murmured Dotty.

"I will go down in history as the greatest scientist

of my age. No, *of all time.* Isaac Newton? An apple fell on your head and you came up with the idea of gravity. **Who cares?** Nicolaus Copernicus? You discovered that the Earth revolves round the Sun rather than the

NEWTON   COPERNICUS   DARWIN

other way round? Big deal! Charles Darwin? So you completely changed the way we think about life on Earth with your theory of evolution? Duh! They will rip up your books, burn your paintings and tear down your statues and put up ones of ME! ME! ME! YES! IT WILL ALL BE ABOUT ME!"

There was an uncomfortable silence for a moment.

"Have you finished?" asked Elsie.

The professor paused for thought. "Yes. You two

will be my assistants. You must do everything I say, and be prepared to lay down your lives in the name of science if need be. Now come on! There's no time to lose."

Instantly, the old man started busying himself about his laboratory, handing pieces of scientific equipment to Elsie, who followed him around like an eager puppy. Dotty looked on in disbelief.

"Have you two completely lost your minds?" she asked.

"The mind is an abstract construct," replied the professor.

"What he just said," agreed the girl, not having understood a word of it.

"If you do manage to catch a bolt of lightning and somehow bring this manmoth…"

"Mammoth," corrected Elsie.

"Manmoth, that is what I said, back to life, what are you going to do with it?"

It was a good question, and stopped both of them in their tracks.

"Mmm," pondered the girl. "Well, maybe the mammoth can come and live with you?"

Dotty went dotty. "With me? I rent a tiny attic room in a boarding house. There's a 'no cats or dogs' rule."

"What about a **'NO MAMMOTHS'** rule?" asked Elsie.

"No!"

"Well then…"

"There ain't a 'no dinosaurs' rule either! I ain't sure the landlady thought she'd need any rules about animals that've been extinct for millions of years."

"Well, if it can't live with you, maybe it can come and live with me," said Elsie.

"You don't have a home."

"So maybe we can set it free."

Elsie noticed the professor smiling to himself. He was hiding something. But what?

"We can work on all the finer details in good time," he said. "First, we have to bring it back to life. Now, where did I put that copper wire?"

Dotty grabbed whatever bit of scientific equipment

Elsie was holding and put it down on the counter.

"Come on, Elsie, this is all going to end in tears," said the lady.

With that, Dotty grabbed the girl's hand and dragged her over to the secret door.

"Please, Dotty, I beg you," cried the professor. "I need your help too!"

"NO!"

"PLEASE!"

"NO MEANS NO!"

Just the other side of the door, bootsteps could once again be heard.

CLICK CLACK CLICK CLACK CLICK CLACK!

The pair fell silent.

"Shush!" hushed Elsie. "It's Clout."

"He doesn't know I'm here," hissed the professor. "Nobody does. If you've led him here, then—"

"Shush!" shushed the girl again.

All three kept dead still as the bootsteps came to a halt right outside the secret door.

CLICK CLACK CLICK CLACK CLICK CLACK!

There followed the sound of light tapping.

TAP TAP TAP…

Dotty held her chest. Her heart was racing.

TAP TAP TAP…

Elsie had had to hide herself countless times before. The trick was not to breathe. The girl stretched out her hand to silence the old lady. Dotty clasped her hands together and closed her eyes in prayer.

TAP TAP TAP…

Had Clout worked out there was something behind the secret door?

Not yet.

There was the sound of bootsteps again, as Clout moved off.

CLICK CLACK CLICK CLACK CLICK CLACK…

"If I know Mr Clout, he will be back," whispered the professor. "We have to move at lightning speed if we want to bring the monster back to life."

"What could possibly go wrong?" muttered Dotty.

· ⭑ ·

Chapter 21

A THOUSAND
SILK HANDKERCHIEFS

In his secret laboratory, the professor expounded his **madcap** plan.

"We need to make a giant hot-air balloon from silk handkerchiefs, and fly it high over the museum into a lightning storm. Elsie, you will need to steal the silk handkerchiefs. Have you ever stolen anything before?"

"Once or twice," lied the girl. "How many do you need?"

"Mmm. No more than a thousand."

"A *thousand?*"

"Give or take."

"Where am I going to get a *thousand* silk handkerchiefs from?"

"A thousand well-to-do ladies and gentlemen, of course. Now, we will also need a round piece of metal," continued the professor. "Like a soldier's tin helmet."

Suddenly Dotty jumped up and down, looking as if she desperately needed a wee, but in actual fact she was just overexcited.

"Ooh! Ooh!" she cried, waving her hand in the air.

"Yes?" asked the professor.

"I know where to get a tin helmet. Me boyfriend, Titch, will have one from his war days."

"Perfect! We will need to attach it to the top of the balloon. Let me show you…"

The professor reached into the pocket of his dirty laboratory coat. "Now where on earth is my chalk?"

Elsie looked a little sheepish. "Oh, it must have slipped out of your pocket and into my hand," she lied.

"Very good, child. Very good!" The professor was mightily impressed. "Those fingers will come in handy when you're stealing the handkerchiefs."

The old man held out his hand and she placed the stolen chalk into it. Then he began drawing his invention on the wall of the laboratory, giving a commentary as he sketched.

"So here is the balloon, with the tin helmet at the very top. The balloon will have a wicker basket attached by ropes at the bottom here. In the middle of the basket, we will place a metal drum. Inside that drum, wood will be burned. The hot air will cause the balloon to inflate and take to the skies."

"Ooh, this is all getting very involved!" muttered Dotty.

"Silence while the great professor speaks!" he

snapped. "Then the pilot of the balloon will fly up into the heart of the storm. When lightning strikes here..."

He bashed his chalk against his drawing of the metal helmet.

"...the lightning bolt will travel along this length of copper wire, all the way down through the museum itself. The end of the wire we will have embedded right into—"

But before he could finish his sentence Elsie did it for him: "The mammoth's heart."

"Exactly!" exclaimed the professor. "You're a fast learner, young lady."

Dotty put her hand in the air.

"Yes?" he asked grandly.

"Can I say something?"

"No!" he snapped.

The lady crossed her arms in a sulk.

"So you, Elsie, will steal the thousand silk handkerchiefs, then you and Dotty will sew them together to make the balloon. The tin helmet this Titch character will provide; the basket, metal drum and firewood Elsie can scavenge from the streets. Copper wire I have here from my last experiment. It couldn't be simpler!"

Dotty and Elsie stood there open-mouthed in shock. "Simple" was not the word that sprang to mind.

"So who will be going up in the balloon?" asked Elsie.

The professor grinned a wicked grin. "Not you, child."

"No?"

"No. I need a little person to squeeze through all the nooks and crannies of the museum and thread that copper wire all the way down from the roof to the main hall."

"Are you going up in the balloon, then, Professor?" asked the girl.

"HA! HA! No, child. My infirmity would prevent me from undertaking such a deadly mission."

"So who is?"

The professor's dark eyes fixed on Dotty. Elsie followed his gaze.

"Why is everyone looking at me?" Dotty asked.

"Because you, cleaning woman, will have the

honour of taking on the most dangerous – perhaps deadly – part of the mission.

Flying the hot-air balloon straight into a lightning storm!"

Chapter 22

◆

THE BEAUTY
OF THE SCHEME

"**M**E?" exclaimed Dotty.

"YES, YOU!" replied the professor.

"But I'm scared of heights. I even feel wobbly standing on a chair to dust the ceiling."

"Listen to me, woman!" commanded the professor. "What better honour could there be in life than to *DIE* in the name of science?"

"*DIE?*"

"That would be the worst-case scenario."

"I'm too young to die."

The professor peered over his half-moon spectacles to examine the lady. "I beg to differ."

"How dare you!"

"I will go up in the balloon!" offered Elsie.

"No, no, no," began the man. "How on earth

would we get this great fat lump down a chimney?"

"Charming!" exclaimed Dotty. "Now I'm old *and* fat?"

"Don't fret, woman. There is little chance of you falling out and plunging to your death, as I can strap you to the basket."

"That's reassuring," replied the lady.

"Obviously, the real danger is being hit by lightning."

"WHAT?"

"Don't worry. It's a very quick and painless *DEATH*. You will be incinerated in a millisecond. You would barely know what hit you. That's the beauty of the scheme."

"You're nuts."

"Thank you," replied the professor.

"What about Clout?" asked Elsie.

"Yes," mused the man. "The security guard can be very troublesome. We need to somehow make sure he's otherwise engaged."

"I don't think he's engaged, or married," said Dotty.

"It's a figure of speech!" exclaimed the professor.

"Perhaps we could lock him in the cleaning cupboard," suggested the girl.

"That would be perfect," he replied.

"How are we going to get out of here without being seen?" asked Elsie. "The whole museum is swarming with police and guards right now."

"You can climb out of the coal chute, just here…"

The man wheeled himself over to the wall, and revealed a small opening hidden by a box.

Dotty examined the hole. "What about me?" she asked.

"You can try and squeeze yourself up the chute and then I can poke you through by prodding your ample bottom with this broomstick."

"That's very kind of you," replied Dotty sarcastically, "but they ain't looking for me. Just the girl. I think I'll wait a while, and then when the coast is clear go out the door and up the stairs."

"Yes, but don't wait too long, please," replied the professor. "I don't want you cluttering up the place."

"Well, excuse me!"

"Elsie?"

"Yes, Professor?"

"I want you back here at this time tomorrow night with *one thousand* silk handkerchiefs."

"Tomorrow night?"

"Yes, child. No later than nine o'clock tomorrow night. And look here, the air pressure is getting lower…" The man pointed to a barometer on the wall. "We need to be ready for a lightning storm by the end of the week."

"I'll do my best, Professor!" said the girl as she shimmied up the chute.

The professor stared at Dotty for a while.

"Are you still here?" he asked.

Meanwhile, Elsie ran away from the museum as fast as she could. Her mind raced along with her legs. How on earth was she going to steal *one thousand handkerchiefs* in just *twenty-four hours?*

Chapter 23

THE STICKY FINGERS GANG

Elsie knew there was no way she could do this all on her own. So she decided to get some help. Expert help. There was a **legendary** group of tearaways who were the best pickpockets in the whole of London. If only she could find them.

They were named the **Sticky Fingers Gang**.

They were so called because their sticky little fingers would worm their way into the coat pockets of every rich lady and gentleman in London, and then worm their way out with things stuck to them.

Sometimes, it would be nothing more than a half-sucked sweet, a snotty rag or – worst of all – a set of false teeth.

However, at other times their fingers would stick themselves to precious things. Things like **pocket watches**, **gold coins**, silver-rimmed spectacles, *jewels* and, of course, *silk handkerchiefs*.

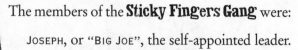

The members of the **Sticky Fingers Gang** were:

JOSEPH, or "BIG JOE", the self-appointed leader. He could pick pockets in his sleep.

ZOE, the real leader. She had been thieving since before she could walk. She was known to readers of *The Times*, who wrote often about her crimes, as the "BABY-FACED BADDY".

NELLIE was better known as "SMELLY NELLIE" as she used her bottom burps to distract her victims.

BELLA, or "LITTLE'UN", was the shortest of the gang. She could barely reach the pockets of the rich ladies and gentlemen of London, so carried a stool around with her to help.

LOTTIE was the baddest of the lot. Pickpocketing was just one of her many crimes. She was wanted by police forces all over England for "duffing up a strongman", "doing a cheesy burp in the face of a nun" and "force-feeding cheese to a nun".

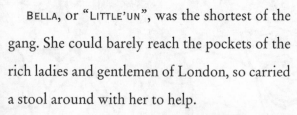

GRACE, or "DANGEROUS GRACE", was the toughest member of the gang. Nobody, but

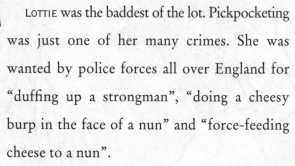

nobody, crossed GRACE, unless they wanted a wedgie, a Chinese burn or a knuckle sandwich.

GEORGE

GEORGE, or "GUILTLESS GEORGE", looked innocent, but he was anything but. GEORGE disguised himself as a choirboy, which meant he could get away with absolute murder.

FREYA

"LIGHT-FINGERED FREYA" could steal for England. One day at a fairground, she stole 318 silk handkerchiefs, a barrel of sugar plums and a carousel.

ASIA

ASIA and ATHENA were sisters, and partners in crime. When they weren't warring with each other, they oversaw a criminal empire that included gambling, extortion and bare-knuckle boxing. They were known as the "SISTERS OF NO MERCY".

ATHENA

Two more sisters rounded off the gang: SANAYA and RIYANA, the "GRUESOME TWOSOME". The pair worked as a team: SANAYA would pose as a sweet flower-seller as her little sister, RIYANA, came round the back and robbed you blind.

SANAYA

RIYANA

The **Sticky Fingers Gang** were legendary figures on the streets of London. Rumours of their exploits swirled across the city. But nobody had a clue where to find them. Except Elsie.

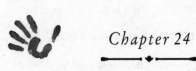

Chapter 24

HANDPRINTS

E lsie had noticed that all over London there were small red handprints on walls and buildings. Once, in the dead of night, she had seen Dangerous Grace put one on the side of St Paul's Cathedral. Elsie was sure it was some kind of secret sign. Some way that the gang communicated with one another. So Elsie had followed Grace as she added more red handprints to the door of 10 Downing Street and even Westminster Abbey.

The handprints looked like arrows, pointing somewhere.

So the night the professor sent Elsie out on her mission she followed the trail all the way to the Houses of Parliament. The last one she found was on the clock tower of Big Ben. It pointed UPWARDS. Surely this

couldn't mean that the **Sticky Fingers Gang's** secret hideout was up there?

There was only one way to find out.

Elsie forced open a tiny door at the base, and climbed up the staircase to the very top of the tower.

"Hello?" called out Elsie as she stepped into the room, the huge clock face looming behind her like a full moon.

BONG! bonged Big Ben.

"Is there anybody there?" asked Elsie.

The girl could swear she heard

scuttling. Maybe it was a rat. Maybe it wasn't.

"Hello? I'm looking for the Sticky Fingers—"

Before she could utter the word "Gang", a cloth bag was thrown over her head.

"HELP!" she screamed.

BONG!

"Shut your face," hissed an unseen voice.

Elsie was hurled into a corner, and she took the bag off her head.

BONG!

A number of children appeared from the shadows.

"What the stink are you doing here?" demanded Big Joe.

BONG!

Zoe pushed him aside. "What are you doing here, little mite? If you want to join our gang, you better think again."

BONG!

The two sisters Sanaya and Riyana pulled Elsie to her feet, then began playing catch with her as if she were a ball.

"Think you're tough enough, do ya?" said the elder one.

"You couldn't punch your way out of a paper bag," added the younger one.

BONG!

Suddenly a shove came from behind. Elsie turned round. It was Grace. The girl yanked Elsie's ear.

"OW!"

"Crybaby!" snorted Grace.

BONG!

George, dressed in his choirboy disguise, stepped forward, wielding a hymn book.

BONK!

He bashed it down on the girl's head.

"OW!"

"OOPS!" he chuckled. "I dropped me hymn book!"

BONG!

Now it was Bella's turn. The little girl marched forward and plonked her stool down in front of Elsie. She climbed on it and then poked Elsie in the eye.

PLONK!

"ARGH!"

BONG!

"You ain't seen nothing, right? Or if you like I can do the other eye?"

"NO, NO, PLEASE..." pleaded Elsie.

BONG!

Then Asia and Athena took their turn, using the girl as a punchbag.

"She's about as tough as a plate of jelly."

"She'll be jelly when we're finished with her."

BONG!

Finally, Nellie stepped forward. She wore heavy boots far too big for her and stamped on the little girl's toes.

DONK!

"AAAHHH!"

BONG!

"Not so tough now, are you?" sneered Nellie. "Why don't you go running back to Mummy?"

Elsie took a deep breath and gathered her thoughts.

"Because, like you, I ain't got no mummy. And, please, I need you to help someone, or rather *something*, that don't have one neither…"

"Something?" asked Zoe.

The **Sticky Fingers Gang** all leaned forward.

Elsie grinned from ear to ear. She had them hooked.

Chapter 25

❖

PICKPOCKETING
ON ICE

This was the best bedtime story ever. Up in the clock tower of Big Ben, Elsie told the gang of child thieves the whole tale. Just as with all the orphans at WORMLY HALL, the girl had the entire audience enthralled with her storytelling. She told them how the mammoth had been found, about Queen Victoria's visit and how the plan was to bring it back to life with a bolt of lightning.

"Let me get this straight," began Big Joe. "You need us to help you steal one *thousand* silk handkerchiefs?"

Elsie nodded her head.

"Well," began Zoe, "that should be all in a day's work for the **Sticky Fingers Gang**."

Indeed, it was. And, for Elsie, the most fun day ever.

London had become so cold that winter that the

River Thames had frozen over. Ladies and gentlemen had put on their skates and were spinning across the ice. The perfect setting for a ballet of pickpocketing. Elsie became part of the most infamous child gang in London for the day, as they swooped and twirled and robbed.

D I N G !

A silk handkerchief.

And another.

D I N G !

And another and another and another.

D I N G !

A toffee apple. Yum.

D I N G !

A box of toenail clippings.

Not so yum.

D I N G !

A silk handkerchief.

D I N G !

Another.

D I N G !

A pair of ladies' bloomers?

What were they doing in a

bishop's pocket?

D I N G !

A Scotch egg.

D I N G !

A silk handkerchief.

D I N G !

Another!

D I N G !

A glove.

D I N G !

A flask of brandy.

D I N G !

A silk handkerchief.

The day went like a

dream.

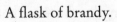

When two policemen made their way across the ice, Elsie assumed that the fun might be over. Far from it. The **Sticky Fingers Gang** were such skilled thieves they simply stole from the policemen too!

DING!

A cheese-and-pickle sandwich.

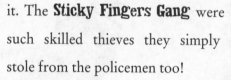

DING!

A pair of handcuffs.

⎯⎯⎯ ◆ ⎯⎯⎯

After a long and surprisingly tiring day of robbing, the gang and Elsie retired to the clock tower to share out the spoils.

"I've lost count of how many 'kerchiefs we got," said Zoe. "But there must be over a *thousand* 'ere! The rest of the loot we'll give to the poor!"

"Yeah! Us!" snorted George.

All the gang laughed.

As for Elsie, her eyes lit up with joy. With the help of her new friends, she had achieved the impossible. Now she could return to the **NATURAL HISTORY MUSEUM** in triumph.

"Good luck, kid," said Bella.

It was strange being called "kid" by someone considerably smaller than you, but Bella was a feisty one and so Elsie let it pass.

"Goodbye," said Elsie as she threw the haul of handkerchiefs over her shoulder, and hurried out of the clock tower as the bell chimed eight times.

BONG! BONG! BONG!
BONG! BONG! BONG!
BONG! BONG!

The girl had done it.

Chapter 26

❖

A LITTLE PROBLEM

Elsie took the thousand silk handkerchiefs and one pair of ladies' bloomers to the professor. Immediately, he put her and Dotty to work sewing them all together to make something that resembled a balloon. The other bits and pieces the professor asked for were gathered together, and by the end of the week the unlikely trio were ready.

As storm clouds gathered over London, the professor decided that tonight was the night to take to the skies. Now was the moment to see if a prehistoric creature that had been *DEAD* for ten thousand years really could be brought back to life.

But, before all that, there was the little problem of Mr Clout. The security guard patrolled the **NATURAL HISTORY MUSEUM** at night and, although he wasn't the brightest spark, there was every chance he would notice a live mammoth.

CLICK CLACK CLICK CLACK CLICK CLACK!

You could hear him coming a mile off in those hobnailed boots of his.

"Good evening, Mr Clout, sir," said Dotty as she pretended to mop the corridor.

"Why are you still here?" asked the security guard. He took pleasure in treading all over the clean part of the floor, so poor Dotty would have to do it all again. It was way past closing time at the museum, and Clout was used to having the place to himself. Dotty should be long gone by now.

"Yes, Mr Clout, sir. And behold. There is a very stubborn stain on the ceiling."

"The ceiling?"

"Yes."

"How would there be a stain on the ceiling?"

"Maybe someone spilled their tea and it went upwards."

"Upwards?"

"It can happen."

Clout peered up. "I can't see anything."

"Keep looking," urged Dotty.

This was Elsie's cue. Unseen by Clout, she crawled between his legs and began untying his long bootlaces.

Dotty stole glances at the girl to check her progress.

"There is no stain," said the man.

"Keep looking!"

Then Elsie began tying his boots together.

"I think you have finally lost your marbles, madam."

"Keep looking."

Elsie nodded to Dotty. That was her cue. The cleaning lady whisked up her bucket and slammed it down over Clout's head.

CLANG!

The man couldn't see a thing.

"Who turned the lights out?"

As his boots were tied together, he couldn't get away.

"QUICK!" shouted Elsie, and together she and Dotty bundled him into the cleaning cupboard.

"GET OFF ME!"

They slammed the door.

DONK!

And locked it.

CLICK!

BOOM! BOOM! BOOM!

Clout thumped on the door. "LET ME OUT!"

Outside the door, the pair giggled like naughty schoolchildren.

"TEE! HEE! HEE!"

"Right," said Elsie, "let's get to work."

. ⚹ .

Chapter 27

THUNDERSNOW

Standing on the top of one of the **NATURAL HISTORY MUSEUM'S** towers, Elsie ordered Dotty to listen.

After a few moments, the lady became restless and asked, "What are we listening for?"

"Silence," replied the girl.

"It's quite hard to hear that."

"Shush!" chided Elsie. "Listen, the birds in the trees have gone quiet."

"You're right," replied Dotty.

Above their heads, black clouds rolled across the sky.

"It feels too cold to rain," said the lady.

"It's not going to rain. It's going to snow. *THUNDERSNOW*. You get to know this stuff when you don't have a roof over your head."

"*THUNDERSNOW?* Sounds very dramatic. Do you think it's safe to be all the way up here during a '*THUNDERSNOW*'?"

"No."

"I thought as much. Oh well, if anything happens to me, please tell Titch I love him."

"Oh yes. Titch."

"You'll find him at the Royal Hospital. He lent us this tin helmet."

"Oh yes. I thought it was tiny."

"Good things come in small packages. Now, I want to leave all my earthly goods, my mops, my brushes and my bucket to you, Elsie."

"That's very kind. I'm touched, Dotty. Truly."

"But if I get a job as a cleaning lady in heaven I'll need them back. Understood?"

"Yes. You can have them back any time you want them, either in this world or the next. Now, let's get this fire going."

They turned their attention to their home-made hot-air balloon, which they had assembled by following the professor's instructions.

After a few attempts, they got the wood in the drum burning. Hot air began to rise. Slowly, the balloon of handkerchiefs (and one pair of bloomers) began to inflate. Miraculously, the stitches held firm.

The multicoloured globe grew and grew until it looked big enough to take Dotty's not-inconsiderable weight.

Elsie turned to Dotty. "Now, when I tug on the copper wire three times, that means the other end is stuck right in the mammoth's heart."

"The manmoth's? Yes."

There wasn't time to correct her, so Elsie ploughed on. "Then, and only then, should you launch the balloon into the air. Understand?"

"Yes. Three times." Dotty nodded.

BOOM!

Thunder echoed across the sky.

To the side of the tower was a narrow chimney pipe. It wasn't much wider than a dinner plate. Elsie breathed out all the air she had inside her, and lowered herself feet first down the chimney.

"See you at the bottom," she called up.

"Aren't you forgetting something?" asked Dotty.

Elsie looked up at the lady, confused. "The wire?"

"Oh yes. That would be useful," said Elsie.

"You're as daft as I am!" chuckled Dotty.

She held out the end of the wire and Elsie placed it in her mouth before disappearing down into the darkness. The girl's hands and feet frantically searched the sides for nooks and crevices to hold on to. Eventually, she could see a tiny square of light beneath her. It was the fireplace that opened into the museum director's office.

SQUAWK!

"Argh!" screamed the girl.

Something was attacking her.

Feathers. A beak. Talons.

A bird! It must have been nesting in the chimney stack.

The creature seemed as frightened as she was. Both were flailing around in a desperate attempt to survive.

In all the commotion, Elsie began sliding down at speed.

"AAAHHH!"

she cried.

Chapter 28

A GIANT CATAPULT

What seemed like a split second later, she was lying in a crumpled heap on the floor of Sir Ray Lankester's oak-panelled office. The girl had brought a cloud of soot with her, and she couldn't help coughing and spluttering as she tried to breathe.

"HUH! HUH! HUH!"

As the cloud passed, she found herself face to face with a horned creature.

"NOOO!"

As her hand reached out to stop it attacking her, she realised it was STUFFED. A plinth underneath read PYRENEAN IBEX (not that Elsie could read).

The girl scrambled to her feet. Although everything hurt, she hadn't broken any bones.

Elsie took the copper wire in her hand and tiptoed over to the door of the office.

She rattled the handle. It was locked!

BLAST! That wasn't part of the plan.

There must be a key somewhere in the room. Elsie opened every drawer, turned every box upside down and swept her hands over every shelf, but she couldn't find it anywhere. There was a cupboard of clothes, and she felt in every pocket, but there was no key.

Elsie looked back at the strange horned creature. It looked back at her. The stuffed Pyrenean ibex was the perfect battering ram.

She leaped on to the creature's back and, using her feet to power it along, slammed against the heavy oak door. It barely made a scratch.

BING!

Elsie had an idea. She returned to the cupboard and pulled out a pair of elasticated braces from some trousers that were hanging there. She tied the ends of the braces to the leg of the heavy desk on one side, and to the door handle on the other. Then she moved the ibex into position, with the braces behind its behind. Using all her might, the mite pulled it as far back as she possibly could.

Elsie had created a giant catapult!

When she couldn't hold it for a moment longer, she let go.

TWANG!

The braces shot the ibex across the office. It smashed through the door.

BOOM!

It sent shards of wood flying through the air.

W H I Z Z !

Elsie couldn't help but smile at the destruction she had caused.

She picked up the end of the copper wire and with a smile on her face waltzed through the hole she had made in the door.

Chapter 29

DINO-LADDER

Down in the main hall, the professor was sitting in his wheelchair, staring up at the **ICE MONSTER**. Frozen air was smouldering from the glass tank. Elsie dashed down the steps to join him.

"The ice! It's melting!" she exclaimed.

"Yes, child. I turned off the cooling system," replied the professor. "Otherwise we would never get the end of that copper wire into the creature's heart."

"But what if we bring it back to life and it immediately drowns in the water?"

"I've thought of that, young lady. That's what *THIS* is for!"

From under his wheelchair, he produced a frightening tool that looked halfway between a hammer and an axe.

"A pickaxe?"

"Yes, child. This will break through the glass. Now, are you ready?"

"Ready for what?"

"To dive into the tank, of course."

"Me?"

"Yes, you."

"I can't swim. What if I drown?"

The professor thought for a moment. "Then, urchin, you will be immortalised."

"Immortalised?"

"Yes, immortalised as a short footnote* in the story of how I, the great professor, brought the **ICE MONSTER** back to life. Now climb to the top of the tank."

Elsie looked around the hall. "Have you got a ladder, Professor?" she asked.

The man's expression darkened. "Oops," he replied. "I forgot that."

"Not so great after all, are you?" mused the girl.

The professor gripped the pickaxe tightly.

"I'll find a way," said Elsie.

---

* *A footnote is a short note written at the bottom of a page, like this.*

She looked around the main hall for something, anything, that could be used as a ladder. Elsie realised that the answer was standing right next to her.

"The *Diplodocus*!" she exclaimed.

The ENORMOUS dinosaur skeleton was towering over her.

"You can climb that?" he asked.

"Yes! I have monkey feet! I'll think of it as a dino-ladder!"

"What a **genius idea** of mine!" announced the professor. "Then, when you reach the tank, you must swim down to the creature's heart."

"I already told you – I can't swim! But I could sink!"

"What do you mean?"

"Professor, may I borrow that pickaxe?"

"Be my guest."

The girl took it from him. It felt really heavy, but she did her best to pretend it wasn't. She marched over to a glass cabinet that housed a rock the size of a football.

CRASH!

She smashed the glass, and heaved out the rock.

"That's a meteorite!" remarked the professor.

"Here you go," she said, passing back the pickaxe. "This meteorite will make me sink."

"What a splendid idea of mine!" he mused.

Elsie placed the end of the copper wire back in her mouth, and picked up the rock. Slowly but surely, her monkey feet began stepping along the bones of the tail.

As if climbing a dinosaur skeleton holding a meteorite weren't hard enough already, it was dark in the museum. The only light was the occasional flash of lightning outside the snow-encrusted windows.

"Quickly!" ordered the professor. "We're going to lose the lightning!"

"I'm going as fast as I can," snapped back the girl.

The bones themselves were smooth, which meant it was very easy to slip on them. Elsie took it slowly, letting her toes grip as tightly as they could. In a short while she had reached the skeleton's back. This being a much wider part, she managed to speed up. Now the girl was at the base of the neck, and a very long way up.

Elsie looked down. That was a mistake. It was a very long way down. Instantly she felt dizzy. She shut her eyes. This just made her feel wobblier.

"Why on earth have you stopped, you pathetic, pathetic child?"

Elsie took a deep breath. A bolt of lightning struck just outside the window, illuminating everything for a split second. The girl knew she had to act now. Still holding the meteorite, she took a step forward, and another and another. Soon she was halfway across the skeleton's neck, and within leaping distance of the mammoth's tank.

BOOM!

A roll of thunder roared across the sky. It was so
loud that the museum shook a little.

It made Elsie's heart skip a beat, and she lost
her footing.

"AAH!" she screamed.

Chapter 30

◆

THE HEART OF THE STORM

E lsie tumbled forward. But, by beautiful chance, the back of her coat hooked on to one of the *Diplodocus* bones. Without even realising quite what had happened, the girl found herself swinging in the air, still miraculously holding on to the meteorite.

"I'm alive!" she exclaimed.

"Yes, I can see that, you foolish child. Now come on, stop dilly-dallying! We haven't got all night."

The girl swung her legs forward and gripped on to the neck bones. With her legs wrapped tightly round the exhibit, she unhooked her coat and swung herself back up using the meteorite for momentum.

The skull of the *Diplodocus* was within

spitting distance of the tank. From there, she LEAPED on to the top.

DOINK!

The tank was freezing, and her toes tingled with the cold.

"Have you found the hatch?" demanded the professor.

Elsie looked ahead. "YES!"

"Unscrew the bolts round the edge."

She put down the meteorite and opened the hatch.

"Now get in, and push the end of the copper wire into the mammoth's heart just where I showed you."

Elsie nodded, picked up the meteorite and plunged down into the icy water.

SPLOSH!

"UH!" she exclaimed. The cold shocked her, and she could hardly breathe. Still holding the meteorite, she sank like a stone. Within a second, she was at the bottom of the tank.

From his wheelchair, the professor frantically pointed out to Elsie where the creature's heart was.

Elsie let go of the meteorite and floated upwards, plunging the end of the copper wire deep into the mammoth's chest. Elsie now felt completely out of breath, and let herself float back up to the top of the tank. Her head bobbing through the hatch, she gasped for air. With her entire body shaking from the cold, she hauled herself up on to the top of the tank. There she lay, soaking wet and shivering, but thankful to still be alive.

"Don't just lie there, child!" the professor called up.

"W-w-what n-n-now?"

"Look outside the window. We're in the middle of a storm. Time is of the essence. You need to tug the wire three times as a signal to Dotty to take off in the hot-air balloon!"

The girl did what she was told.

TUG! TUG! TUG!

Next, Elsie leaped off the tank back on to the *Diplodocus* skeleton. Within moments the length of wire tightened.

"PERFECT!" called out the professor.

Up on the roof of
the museum, a cold and
miserable Dotty finally got
the signal. As fast as she could,
she untied the ropes that were
holding the basket down, and took
to the skies.

WHOOSH!

The lady was flying straight into the
HEART of the storm.

Soon bolts of lightning were exploding all
around her.

 BOOM! BOOOM! **BOOOOM!**

Against her better judgement, she steered the
balloon into their path and…

BANG!

…a rush of electricity struck the tin helmet on top
of the balloon.

TING!

The copper wire glowed as energy shot through it.

SIZZLE!

"Oh no," whispered Dotty
to herself. "I think a bit of wee
came out!"

The bolt of lightning sped all the way down the wire,
to the tower, down the chimney, across the director's
office, along the corridor, round a corner, down the
steps and into the tank. The punch of electricity hit the

mammoth straight in the heart.

They had done it.

Or had they?

The professor and Elsie looked on as nothing happened.

Nothing at all.
Nought.
Zero.

Zilch.

"NO! It hasn't worked!" raged the professor.

"Wait," whispered the girl. "I can sense something's changed."

Elsie put her hand up to the glass, and looked deep into the mammoth's eye.

Unless her mind was playing tricks on her, she was sure the creature was staring straight back at her.

Then the most incredible thing happened.

It blinked.

"Did you see that, Professor?" exclaimed Elsie.

"What?"

"It blinked!"

In his wheelchair, the professor began shaking with excitement. He took a deep breath, before proclaiming,

"IT'S ALIVE!"

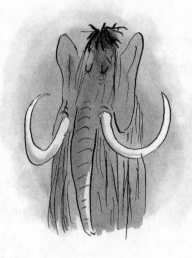

Chapter 31

◆

DON'T LOOK ROUND

E lsie threw her arms round the man, and hugged him tight.

"We did it!" she exclaimed.

"Yes! I did it!" he purred. "Now release me this instant."

The celebration had come too soon, because the mammoth had started thrashing around inside the tank!

It let out a cry, muffled by the water. **"HOOO!"**

If they didn't get the creature out, and soon, it would drown.

The professor wheeled himself over and lifted the pickaxe above his head, before smashing it against the glass.

CRUNCH!

A patchwork of cracks appeared in the glass.

"HOO!" cried the animal under the water.

The creature lurched forward and hit the glass with its tusks.

SMASH!

All at once, the glass fell away, and icy water flooded the main hall, sweeping Elsie off her feet and the professor off his wheels.

SWISH!

"Argh!" screamed the girl as she was hurled against the stone staircase.

DOOF!

The professor had banged his head badly, and was now lying face down in the water, his wheelchair on its side a few feet away from him.

"Professor! Professor?" pleaded the girl.

Suddenly, the old man's eyes opened, and then widened.

"Whatever you do," he began, "don't look round."

Of course, there is nothing like being told not to look round to make you look round.

Slowly, the girl turned her head.

Just behind her was the mammoth, rearing up on its hind legs.

"HOO!"

The instant those legs crashed down, Elsie and the professor would be dead.

· ⚹ ·

Chapter 32

❖

KNOCKED AWAKE

Elsie wrenched the professor out of the way just in time before the mammoth's giant feet thumped on the floor.

SMASH!

"HOOO!" it cried.

"Why is it trying to kill us?" yelled the girl. "We just brought it back to life!"

"It's a wild beast!" replied the professor. "It's not going to say 'thank you'! Now, for goodness' sake, HELP ME!"

Elsie grabbed the old man under his armpits, and pulled him up the huge stone staircase that led upwards through the main hall. When the pair were a few steps up, the mammoth spun round and smashed into the *Diplodocus* skeleton.

CRASH!

Elsie ducked as the giant bones came thundering down all around them.

WHACK!

One struck the professor across the forehead, and knocked him out cold.

DOOF!

"PROFESSOR!" shouted Elsie. The girl slapped the old man across the face to wake him. When that didn't work, she dragged him further up the stairs to escape the animal.

The mammoth began pacing towards them. It reached the bottom of the steps just as Elsie had managed to drag the professor halfway up.

Surely the creature could not follow them up the stairs?

To Elsie's horror, it could.

"NO!" cried the girl.

Unsteadily, the mammoth rested its giant feet on the first step, then the second, then the third.

THUD! THUD! THUD!

In a rush to flee further up the steps, Elsie dropped the professor. His head hit the stone.

CLONK!

Normally, this would have been enough to knock someone out, but as he was already knocked out it actually had the opposite effect. It knocked him **awake.**

"Ouch!" he cried.

"You're awake!" replied Elsie.

"Have I missed anything?"

"We're still going to die."

"Oh no."

"HOOO!"

The mammoth let out its distinctive cry again, its trunk aloft and its sharp tusks now inches from the pair's faces. The creature whisked its head back, as if getting ready to impale them.

"HELP!" cried the girl.

Just then, there was a mighty smash overhead.

KERBANG!

Dotty had crashed her hot-air balloon straight through the newly repaired stained-glass window of the main hall.

SMASH!

It descended at speed through the hall. The bottom of the wicker basket struck the mammoth hard on the head.

BOOF!

"HOOO!"

This cry sounded different. Like a cry of fear. The mammoth scuttled back down the steps and across the main hall to hide under the shadow of an archway.

Meanwhile, the basket landed with a thud and skidded across the floor, until it came to a sudden stop against the wall.

CRASH!

"OOF!" said Dotty. As the cleaning lady scrambled to her feet, she surveyed the scene. There were the scattered dinosaur bones, the shards of glass from the window and the tank, the pools of icy water, the broken basket and the hot-air balloon made of a thousand handkerchiefs and one pair of bloomers strewn across the floor.

"Naughty manmoth!" exclaimed Dotty. "Look at this mess! It will take me all night to clear this up!"

"Idiotic woman! That is the least of our troubles!" interrupted the professor. "The beast just tried to kill us. Isn't that right, Elsie? Elsie?"

The professor looked over his shoulder, but the girl had gone.

"Elsie?" he called. "ELSIE?"

Unknown to him, the girl had made her way over to the archway to take a closer look at the mammoth.

"KEEP BACK, YOU FOOLISH CHILD!" shouted the professor.

"Shush!" shushed the girl. "You're frightening it."

"Whatever you do, don't touch it!" shouted the professor.

The brave little girl ignored him, and reached out her hand to meet the creature's trunk. It was the only part of the mammoth that was not hidden in the darkness.

First, its trunk performed a little dance around the girl's hand, like a snake being charmed. Then Elsie held

out her hand flat, and something magical happened.
The prehistoric met the modern.

The two touched.

Chapter 33

❖

WHAT'S IN A NAME?

"**I**t's beautiful," whispered the girl.

Little by little, Elsie was gaining the creature's trust. At first, her hand only touched the end of the mammoth's trunk for a moment. The animal would retreat, before the girl would try again. Then, as gently as she could, so as not to startle it, she began stroking the fur on its trunk. The animal pressed against her a little. Elsie took this as a prompt to continue. So she started doing longer strokes, branching out to pats on its cheeks. The animal recoiled. Elsie realised her hand was too near the mammoth's eye, so moved it further away. She even tried a tickle under the chin, because stray cats always liked that. Just like the stray cats, the mammoth *PURRED* a little.

Behind Elsie, the two grown-ups were edging closer

to take a look, the professor back in his wheelchair and Dotty pushing him. Neither one could believe their eyes.

"It's extraordinary," muttered the professor. "There's a special connection between them."

"Like me and me favourite mop," added Dotty.

"I think it just misses its ma, that's all," whispered the girl. Then she spoke to the mammoth. "Don't you worry. I'll look after you. I promise."

Although the animal couldn't understand the words, it did understand the feeling. Elsie spoke in soothing tones and, with all the strokes and tickles too, the mammoth could sense the girl's kindness.

"This is history being made!" boasted the professor. "History all about me! The greatest scientist of the age. Nay! Of all time!"

Dotty rolled her eyes. "Here we go again."

"I, and I alone, have brought the dead back to life! I am the real-life Doctor Frankenstein, and this is my monster!"

The professor lifted his hand to touch the mammoth. Instantly, the creature retreated into the darkness.

"It's not a monster!" replied Elsie. She slid under the mammoth for a quick look. "It's a SHE! And she's not yours. She's not anybody's! We've set her free!"

"I don't care if this thing likes me or not!"

"It seems awful calling it a 'thing'!" chimed in Dotty. "She needs a name."

Elsie and Dotty thought for a moment.

"WOOLLY!" exclaimed the girl.

"You can't call it 'Woolly'!" replied the professor.

"Why not?" asked Dotty.

"No, no, no," scoffed the man. "It's boring! Far too obvious. It's like calling a dog 'Doggy'!"

"That's a good name for a dog," replied Dotty. "I wish I'd thought of that. I called mine 'Catty'."

"Heaven help us!" said the professor.

"Well, let's vote on it," steamed in Elsie.

"Women don't have the vote," snapped the man.

The girl grimaced. "Not yet, no, but we can vote on this."

"How?" he asked.

"Because I say so. Now, hands up if you want to name this mammoth 'Woolly'," said Elsie.

The two ladies put a hand up each.

"Looks like you're outvoted, Professor," sniggered the girl.

"DARN AND BLAST!" he thundered.

"What did you want to call her?" asked Dotty.

"I wanted to name it after me!"*

"Well, that's a surprise," mused the lady.

---

* *Many things are named after the people who made them famous. For example, the wellington boot is named after the Duke of Wellington.*

"'The professor'?" asked Elsie, her face screwed up in confusion.

"No, no, no. The Professor Osbert Bertram Cuthbert Farnaby Beverly Smith mammoth!"

"That's a mouthful," remarked Dotty. "No. It would take too long to say. She's called Woolly, and that's that."

"Not fair!" he snapped.

"And don't try and touch her, Oswald Barnaby Custard Beatrice whatever your stupid name is. She doesn't like you," said Elsie. "WOOLLY? WOOLLY?"

The girl held out her hand again, and slowly the animal's trunk uncurled out of the darkness. She touched the tip, and ran her hand down it again.

"She must be peckish!" remarked Dotty. "I'd be peckish if I'd been asleep for ten thousand years. Shall I make her a nice cheese-and-pickle sandwich?"

"Mammoths don't eat cheese-and-pickle sandwiches," snapped the professor.

---

* Sandwiches are named after the fourth Earl of Sandwich, whose idea they were.

"Ham-and-pickle?"

"NO! They don't have ham-and-pickle either. They don't have any type of sandwiches. Sandwiches* weren't invented until a hundred years ago."

"All right, brainbox. What do manmoths eat, then?" pressed Dotty.

"They are herbivores!" replied the professor.

"Herbie-who?" spluttered the lady.

"Grass! Leaves! Plants! And lots of them!"

"Well, we'd better get her to the park, then," said Elsie.

The professor shook his head. "We can't take this creature outside into the world!"

"Why ever not?" asked the girl.

"BECAUSE IT BELONGS IN A CAGE."

Chapter 34

CAGE

"A cage?" exclaimed the girl. "You can't put Woolly in a cage!"

The mammoth must have picked up on the conflict between the two humans, and hid behind Elsie. (Hid as much as a mammoth can hide behind a little girl. Which is **not** very much.)

"Yes, a cage. It's the safest place for a dangerous creature like this," he replied. With that, he wheeled himself over to a spot near the main entrance to the hall, and pulled a lever.

A trapdoor opened and a huge metal cage rose up out of the floor.

CLUNK! CLANK! CLINK!

The noise echoed around the hall, causing the mammoth to move further away into the darkness.

With a huge THUD, the trapdoor closed.

"Look!" said the professor proudly. "I have food and water for the beast in there." He indicated two troughs on the side of the cage.

"It's barely bigger than she is!" protested the girl.

"It will be safe in there. Trust me."

Elsie was glowing with fury. "I don't trust you one bit. That wasn't part of the plan."

"Did you really believe I would set this ten-thousand-year-old creature free to roam the streets of London?"

"But I, I, er…" For once, Elsie was lost for words.

Dotty stood by her side. "All this girl wanted to do was set Woolly free!" she exclaimed.

"The monster is free," began the professor. "**Free** from the ice. **Free** from the grave of history. **Free** to live out the rest of its days in this cage. But it won't be **free** to see her. Oh no! I'll be able to open my very own prehistoric zoo. The only one in existence. **I'll be able to charge a fortune.** A hundred pounds a view. People will come from all over the world to see **the monster.**"

"YOU'RE THE MONSTER!" seethed Elsie. "I would never have done all this if I'd known this was your plan!"

"I assumed as much, child. Which is why I thought I would keep this part of the plan a secret until you outlived your usefulness. Thank you. And goodnight. You may go."

"You can't do this to us!" yelled the girl.

"I just have," was the reply. The professor rolled himself across the hall to the cage, and pulled out a handful of grass. He shook it in his hand. *"Come on, Professor Osbert Bertram Cuthbert Farnaby Beverly Smith mammoth. Dinnertime!"*

The mammoth did not budge, and the professor's face soured. From a leather pouch on his wheelchair, he produced a pistol.

"Maybe this will persuade it," he said as he pointed it at the mammoth.

Elsie stood right in front of Woolly.

"You'll have to kill **me** first!" she said.

Chapter 35

ETERNAL SLEEP

"Oh, and me!" added Dotty, taking up a slightly safer position right behind the girl.

"Why would you bring this beautiful creature back to life only to murder her?" demanded Elsie.

"This gun fires darts, not bullets," replied the professor. "They're tipped with a powerful sleeping drug that can knock an elephant out in seconds."

"And what about a person?" asked Elsie, feeling more than a little frightened.

The professor smirked to himself. "It would put a human being to sleep forever."

"So you're going to kill us until we're *DEAD*?" asked Dotty.

"That doesn't really make sense, but, in short, yes," he replied, now pointing his pistol straight at her.

"You evil, evil man," said the girl.

"Thank you," he replied.

"If you have to kill me, so be it," said Elsie. "Woolly can't be kept in a cage for the rest of her life."

"You can't stop me, child."

"Maybe I can," said Dotty.

The lady reached beside her for what was left of the hot-air balloon's basket. With all her might, she shoved it across the floor of the main hall towards the professor.

W H I Z Z !

He quickly spun his wheelchair out of the way, and the basket smashed against the wall.

DOOF!

"You'll have to do better than that," he purred. "Much better."

Elsie picked up one of the *Diplodocus* bones that the mammoth had helpfully rearranged across the floor.

"How about this?" she asked, wielding it in his direction.

"Goodbye forever, urchin," he said, pointing the gun at her chest.

The professor pulled the trigger.

PPPFFFTTT!

Thinking fast, Elsie whisked the bone up to defend herself. The dart stuck into it.

TWANG!

"HA HA!" said the girl.

"Don't you worry, child. I have plenty more darts. Plenty more."

Immediately, he began fumbling in his pouch for another. This bought precious time for the pair. Elsie picked up one side of the balloon.

"QUICK!" she shouted to Dotty. The lady followed suit and they ran towards the professor and threw it over him like a huge sheet.

WHOOSH!

"GET THIS THING OFF ME!"

he yelled from underneath the one thousand silk handkerchiefs and one pair of ladies' bloomers.

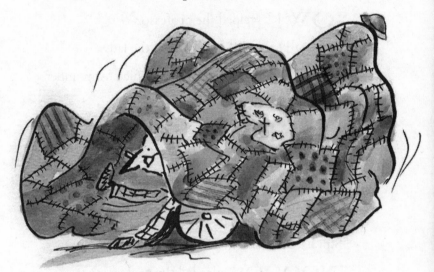

"NOW BASH HIM OVER THE HEAD WITH THE DINO BONE!"

shouted Dotty.

Elsie had never bashed anyone over the head before, and certainly not with a dinosaur bone, but there was a first time for everything. The girl rushed over, and then stood beside the flailing figure, unsure what to do next.

"WHACK HIM!" ordered Dotty.

Elsie did what she was told.

DONK!

"OW!" yelped the professor.

"Not hard enough!" complained the lady.

"YES, IT WAS!" came a muffled voice from under the balloon.

"HARDER!"

Another whack.

DOONNK!

"OWW!"

"Still harder!" said Dotty.

"NOOOO!" pleaded the professor.

"Third time lucky," muttered Elsie. With all her might, she whacked the man over the head with her bone.

DOOONNNKKK!

This time the professor did not cry out, but instead slumped in his wheelchair.

SLUD!

"That might have been too hard," remarked Dotty.

Elsie looked up at the massive hole in the stained-glass window that Dotty had crashed through. The snowstorm had passed, and night was slowly becoming day.

"We need to get Woolly out of here," said Elsie. "And fast."

They looked around, but the mammoth had gone.

"Oh no," said Dotty. "We've only gone and lost her!"

Chapter 36

◆

MISSING
MAMMOTH

You might think a mammoth would be too big to lose, but that was exactly what Elsie and Dotty had done.

"WOOLLY!" called out the girl.

"I'm not sure she's going to come running like a dog," said the lady.

"She can't have gone far."

Elsie looked at the floor of the museum for any mammoth footprints. There was a trail of them that went all the way up the steps.

"She's gone upstairs!" said the girl.

"Oh no," said Dotty. "I cleaned the upper floors last night."

"Why would she have gone up there?"

The lady thought for a moment.

240

"Maybe she wanted to see the butterfly collections?"

Elsie shook her head. "Come on, let's go upstairs and look."

Apart from the sound of the wind, swirling in from the broken windows, the museum was eerily silent. The pair followed the footprints all the way up to the top floor, where they came to a stop outside the library.

"I didn't know manmoths could read," remarked Dotty.

Elsie shook her head in disbelief. "Where to next?"

"Well, this is the top floor of the museum. She can't have got all the way up to…"

Before Dotty could say "the roof", there was a deafening sound from above.

CRASH!

The pair looked at each other. No words were needed.

BOOM!

Debris started falling from the ceiling.

"How do we get on to the roof from here?" asked the girl.

"This is the only way. Follow me."

They scrambled up a flight of steps.

Ahead of them they could see a mammoth-sized hole in the wall.

"More mess!" muttered Dotty.

When they reached the hole, they saw the most startling sight. The mammoth was standing on the roof, looking across London's skyline as dawn was breaking.

It would have been a magnificent scene to paint, but sadly there just wasn't time right now.

"WOOLLY!" cried the girl as she stepped out on to the roof. "What are you doing up here?"

The animal chose to do the same selective hearing trick on Elsie that the girl did on grown-ups. She kept staring forward.

"What is she looking at?" asked Dotty.

Elsie followed the creature's gaze. "The Royal Albert Hall? Hyde Park? Lord's Cricket Ground?"

"Do manmoths like cricket?" asked Dotty.

"I don't imagine so."

"No. Hard to hold the bat with a trunk," she mused.

"What's beyond Lord's?" asked Elsie. She hadn't ventured too far out of central London.

"Hampstead Heath?" replied Dotty.

"Beyond that?"

"Highgate Hill."

"Beyond that?"

"I dunno. I never did History at school."

"Geography!"

"That neither!"

Elsie stood beside Woolly, and patted her side gently. "What are you looking at, my friend?" she whispered to the animal, but the mammoth just kept staring straight ahead.

She lifted her trunk to the sky and let out a
mournful cry.

"HOO!"

The girl wrapped her arms round the animal to give
her a hug. The mammoth leaned towards Elsie, and
wrapped her trunk round her.

"Not too close to the edge, please, Woolly," she
said, guiding the mammoth back.

Dotty took a step forward.

"It's an awfully long way down!" said the lady.

"There's the robber!" came a shout from
the ground.

Elsie looked down over the edge of the roof.

There was a whole squad of policemen looking
up at them.

Chapter 37

❖

BANG! BANG! BANG!

"GET DOWN FROM THERE!" came a shout.

Elsie knew that voice. It was the head of the police, Commissioner Barker.

"We've had reports of a large lady in a hot-air balloon crashing through the window of the museum."

"It wasn't me!" called Dotty. "It must have been another large lady flying a hot-air balloon!"

"Pull the other one! It's got bells on it!" came the shout from below.

Elsie was shaking. "Dotty! If they catch us, they'll lock us up, and goodness knows what they'll do to Woolly."

"Oh dear. Oh dear, oh

dear. Oh dear, oh dear, oh dear."

"Please stop saying 'oh dear' over and over again. We need to find a way out of here or we're all done for!"

"Oh dear!" The poor lady couldn't help it. "Oh dear, I didn't mean to say 'oh dear'. Oh dear."

"YOU HAVE TEN SECONDS TO GIVE YOURSELVES UP OR WE WILL BE FORCED TO OPEN FIRE!" barked Barker. Then there was the sound of rifles being cocked.

CLICK! CLICK! CLICK!

"Have you ever ridden a horse?" asked Elsie.

"No."

"A donkey?"

"No."

"TEN!"

"Ever sat on a carousel at the fair?"

"Oh no."

"Me neither. But how hard can it be?"

"NINE!"

"Are you thinking what I'm thinking?" asked Dotty.

"EIGHT!"

"What am I thinking?" replied the girl.

"SEVEN!"

"That you're going to ride on my back?"

"SIX!"

"I'm **not** thinking that," said Elsie.

"FIVE!"

"Oh dear."

"FOUR!"

"I'm thinking we're going to have to ride this mammoth out of here."

"THREE!"

"Oh dear."

"TWO!"

"Yes, I know. Oh dear. But right now we don't have much choice."

"ONE!"

"Yes!" agreed Dotty.

The pair grabbed hold of a tusk each, and with all their might forced the mammoth backwards, away from the edge of the roof.

"FIRE AT WILL!" came the bellow from down below.

Gunshots crackled in the dawn sky.

BANG!   **BANG!**

BANG!   **BANG!**

. — ⚹ — .

Chapter 38

A SLAP ON THE BOTTOM

BANG! BANG! BANG! BANG! BANG! BANG! BANG! BANG! BANG! BANG! BANG! BANG!

"**HOO!**" The mammoth started wailing. Being a prehistoric creature, she had never heard gunfire before. She began flailing around in fear.

"**AH!**" cried Dotty.

"**HOLD ON!**" yelled Elsie.

The pair gripped on to the tusks as tightly as they could.

"**DON'T LET GO!**"

shouted the girl.

If they did, they would be hurled from the roof, and become human jam on the ground below.

BANG! BANG! BANG! BANG! BANG! BANG! BANG! BANG! BANG! BANG! BANG!

The mammoth retreated through the hole in the wall she had created. Now she was inside the museum, dragging her two new friends with her.

Safely inside, Elsie let go of the tusk, and fell to the floor.

DOOF!

Meanwhile, Dotty was being thrown around like a rag doll.

"HELP!" she shrieked.

"LET GO!"

"WHAT?"

"I SAID 'LET GO'!"

Finally, Dotty did so, and fell face down.

BOOF!

"This floor needs a good polish," she remarked.

"There isn't time for that!" said the girl. "We need to escape!"

BANG! BANG! BANG! BANG! BANG!
BANG! BANG! BANG! BANG! BANG! BANG!
BANG!

"RELOAD!" ordered Barker.

The gunfire had ended for a moment, and the mammoth stopped flailing around. The girl patted the animal, and stroked the fur on her trunk, which helped calm her down.

"Woolly, I will never let anything bad happen to you, I promise," she whispered. "But you're going to have to trust me, all right? I know you're not going to like it at first, but this is the only way out of here. Now, Dotty, give me a leg-up!"

"Are you sure this is a good idea?"

"No, but it's our only idea."

Elsie put her hand on the lady's shoulder. Dotty cupped her own hands, and the girl used them as a step to climb on to the animal's back.

"Good mammoth!" said Elsie. The girl gripped the animal's flanks with her legs, and used two handfuls of fur as reins. To her surprise, the mammoth didn't buck, or even let out a sound. In fact, she immediately seemed comfortable with this new arrangement. Elsie reached out her hand to help Dotty up.

"COME ON!" ordered the girl.

The lady was getting on a bit, and struggled to heave herself up. Once she had, Dotty couldn't swing her leg over the animal like Elsie. Instead, she lay face down on Woolly's back, her head buried in the animal's fur. It all looked rather undignified.

"Are you comfortable?" asked Elsie.

"Of course not," replied Dotty. "But I think we'd best get a move on."

"If you're sure."

The girl had seen the great and the good ride their horses through the parks of London, which had given her some idea of how it might be done. So she dug her heels into the animal's sides, tugged on her fur and ordered, *"GIDDY UP!"*

Unfortunately, the mammoth didn't move an inch.

"Oh dear," muttered Dotty unhelpfully.

"Dotty?" asked the girl.

"Yes, child?"

"Would you mind giving our prehistoric friend a little PAT on the bottom?"

"If you're sure."

"As gently as you can, just to see if we can make her move."

"Understood."

Then the lady did as she was asked. She raised her hand a touch, and brought it down on the animal's rear end.

SLAP!
"HOO!"

Instead of a nice gentle trot, the mammoth went straight into a gallop.

"WOO-HOO!" cried Elsie as they charged down the stairs.

Chapter 39

AN UNWELCOME SIGHT

Poor Dotty was thrown up and down with each step the mammoth took.

POUND! POUND! POUND!

"OOF! OOF! OOF!"

As they rode down the staircase on Woolly's back,

Elsie and Dotty were met by an unwelcome sight. The professor had come to. Now he was sitting up straight in his wheelchair at the bottom of the stairs, with the dart gun in his hand.

"You should have hit me harder," he purred.

"I wish I had now," replied Elsie.

Because of her undignified position, slumped over the back of the animal with her face buried in Woolly's fur, Dotty was struggling to keep up with what was going on.

"Oh no, not him again!" she remarked.

"Prepare to *DIE*. Both of you," said the professor. He pointed the gun straight at Dotty's bottom.

A deafening sound came from the huge wooden doors behind him.

BO**O**M!

"What's that?" asked Elsie.

"That will be the policemen battering their way in," replied the professor.

BO**O**M!

And another.

"There's just enough time to kill you, and claim this monster as mine!"

BO**O**M!

Another!

"I'm going to enjoy this!"

BO**OOOOOO**M_{MM}!

Behind the professor, the doors to the museum burst open.

SMASH!

Shards of wood flew into the air.

The battering ram, which was a huge log on wheels, was going at such a speed the policemen couldn't stop it.

WHIRR!

It sped right towards the professor, whacking the back of his wheelchair.

BOOF!

"ARGH!"

The force of the whack sent the man shooting across the floor.

WHIZZ!

He crashed straight into a glass case of stuffed apes.

BANG!

The professor was thrown up out of his wheelchair...

POW!

...and smashed through the glass.

SHATTER!

Knocked out cold, he landed right between two of the apes. With his mouth wide open, he could have passed for one of them.

All this commotion startled the mammoth, who let out a gigantic…

"HHHHOOOO!"

Elsie patted the animal, and said, "Whoa there, Woolly!"

It was no use; the mammoth began charging towards the line of policemen at the door. The officers all cried out…

"HELP!"

"NOOO!"

"I DON'T BELIEVE IT!"

"IT'S ALIVE!"

"THE ICE THINGUMMY!"

"A REAL-LIFE MONSTER!"

"I AIN'T DONE NO TRAINING FOR MONSTERS!"

"I WANT PAID OVERTIME FOR THIS!"

"MY MA SAID I HAD TO BE BACK FOR BREAKFAST!"

...as they leaped out of the way of the rampaging beast.

Elsie and Dotty held on for their lives as the mammoth galloped out of the museum.

"AFTER THEM, YOU FOOLS!" snarled Barker. "THAT MONSTER IS THE PROPERTY OF THE QUEEN! WE MUST BRING IT BACK ALIVE OR DEAD!"

Chapter 40

CHOCOLATE BALLS

Woolly was way too fast for the policemen. By the time they had scrambled to their feet, the mammoth was long gone. The creature galloped out of the grounds of the NATURAL HISTORY MUSEUM, and charged down the road.

"HOO!"

Try as she might, Elsie could not get the animal to slow down. Poor Dotty was thrown around on the back of the mammoth.

"OOF! OOF! OOF!"

London was waking up, and a handful of market stallholders were wheeling their produce along the snow-covered roads.

"Mind me plums!" shouted one as his barrow of fruit was trampled underfoot.

"Watch me nuts!" yelled another as his roasted chestnuts were sent flying.

"You've crushed my chocolate balls!" hollered a familiar voice.

"That must be Raj," remarked Dotty.

"Who?" asked Elsie.

"Raj! He sells sweets at the market here," replied Dotty. She called out to him. **"HELLO, RAJ!"**

The man smiled and waved. "Oh! Hello, Miss Dotty, my favourite customer! I have some half-chewed liquorice on special offer today!"

"I CAN'T STOP, RAJ!"

"And feel free to come back with that huge furry long-nosed donkey of yours for a sugar lump."

"SHE'S A MANMOTH!"

"She's very big for a moth!"

Still the mammoth galloped through the snow.

"HOOO!" she cried.

"Where's she taking us?" asked Dotty.

"I don't know!" replied Elsie. "But, wherever we're going, we're going to get there fast!"

With some difficulty, Dotty lifted her head to see for herself.

"North!" she exclaimed. "We're heading north!"

"Always north!" replied the girl.

Up ahead, Elsie saw the sandwich-board man she'd met outside the NATURAL HISTORY MUSEUM. On spotting the mammoth charging towards him, he shouted, "THE BEAST IS ALIVE! THE END IS NIGH!"

"Your end will be nigh if you don't get out of the way!" shouted Elsie.

By tugging on the mammoth's fur, the girl just

managed to make her swerve past him.

"THE END IS NOT QUITE NIGH!" he shouted as they passed.

"Woolly's going to trample someone to death if we're not careful," said Elsie. "We need to get her off the streets, hide her somewhere."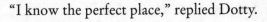

"I know the perfect place," replied Dotty.

"Where?"

"The Royal Hospital. It's not far. It's where Titch lives. He'll help us."

"How do we get there?"

"Can you steer?"

"A little bit."

"Then steer right."

The girl tugged on the fur on the mammoth's right side, and the animal veered right.

"But, Dotty, we can't just turn up there with a mammoth!"

The lady was stumped by this. "Oh yes, you're

right. I'm pretty sure they only treat old soldiers. Not animals."

"Prehistoric animals!"

"Yes. I imagine they aren't welcome."

"Someone might tell on us."

"We have to disguise her somehow!" said the girl.

"We could shave her and say she's an elephant."

"Hold on!"

"I am holding on, love! For dear life!"

"I've got an idea."

Elsie steered the mammoth down a dingy backstreet. Just ahead was a laundry where a number of sheets were hanging up to dry.

"We just need to borrow these sheets."

"Whatever for?"

"You'll see."

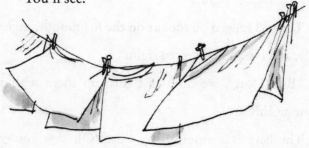

Chapter 41

GOOD EYE

"**I**T'S A WHAT?" roared the guard at the gate of the Royal Hospital. He was a fearsome old soldier, a sergeant major no less, with a chest full of medals on his scarlet coat. He sported a monocle on his left eye, and an eyepatch on his right.

"It's a brand-new top-secret tank!" replied Elsie, gesturing at the mammoth hidden under some sheets.

"**BALDERDASH!**"

"It's not balderdash! It's a brand-new weapon. For Private Thomas," added Dotty.

"Titch Thomas?"

"Yes, that's him! The shortish one."

"Shortish is an understatement!" chortled the sergeant major. "Titch is so tiny he gets mistaken for a toy soldier! Ha! Ha!"

Dotty started to look angry. She didn't appreciate hearing the love of her life spoken about in this manner. "He may be small, but he is perfectly formed!"

"Titch is seventy-three if he's a day," replied the sergeant major. "And his feet wouldn't reach the pedals! What on earth does he need this contraption for?"

"That's top secret, isn't it?" answered Elsie. "If we told you, it wouldn't be top secret."

The old soldier did not look convinced. "Who are you, anyway?"

"That's top secret too!" replied the girl.

"Now open this gate!" ordered Dotty.

"HOO!" went the mammoth. From under the sheet, she raised her trunk. The sergeant major was becoming increasingly suspicious.

Elsie and Dotty looked at each other nervously.

"What was that?" demanded the sergeant major.

"That?" asked Dotty.

"Yes, that!"

"Erm, um, well…" began Elsie. "It was its cannon thing, just lifting up."

She pushed down on the trunk, and Woolly let out another **"HOO!"**

"It just said something!" snarled the sergeant major.

"No, it didn't!"

"Yes, it did!"

"Didn't!"

"Did!"

"It was me!" chimed in Dotty.

"I was looking at you the whole time," said the old soldier.

"From the good eye?"

"Yes! From the good eye! Your face didn't move."

"Well," began Dotty. "That's because…"

"Spit it out, woman!"

"That's because the sound came from… my botty."

"Your botty, madam?"

.–⁑–.

Chapter 42

◆

BACK-DOOR BARRAGE

"It was a botty burp!" explained Dotty.

"I can't smell anything!" protested the sergeant major, pointing his nose towards the lady and sniffing the air.

"Count yourself lucky!" chimed in Elsie, continuing the lie by wafting the air in front of her screwed-up face. "POOH! IT'S A REAL STINKER."

"How utterly uncouth," huffed the old soldier. "I had no idea that ladies could even, for want of a more polite expression, unleash a gas attack."*

"Sadly, it happens," mused Dotty.

"HOO!"

"There my bottom goes again!"

---

* Other military terms for breaking wind the sergeant major could have used include: one-gun salute, bottom blast, invisible grenade, dirty bomb, back-door barrage, attack from the rear.

"HOOOOO!"

"Oops, and again!"

The sergeant major's face turned a shade of beetroot.

"Madam, do you have any control over your, for want

of a more polite expression, rear gun?"

"HOOOO!"

"It seems not," replied Dotty. "Dotty's gotty a

grotty botty."

Elsie could feel the mammoth becoming more and more restless. "Please let us through before she lets another one go!"

"Most irregular!" muttered the old soldier. He raised the gate at once, and saluted as the three unlikely visitors passed through into the grounds of the Royal Hospital.

"Thank you so much," said Elsie.

"HOOOO!"

"Naughty bottom!" called out Dotty, slapping her own rear end.

Just as they led the mammoth across the lawn, she stopped. With her trunk, she snuffled under the snow, and began to munch on the frozen grass.

"RUMPH! RUMPH! RUMPH!"

Having not eaten for ten thousand years, the animal was hungry. As much as the pair tried to keep moving, the mammoth was staying put. From under the sheets she munched and munched and munched. She must have eaten a ton of grass before she was full.

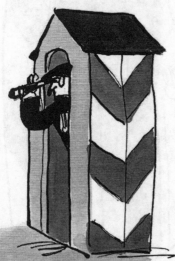

From his sentry post, the sergeant major looked on. He raised a telescope to his good eye, and spied on the strange goings-on in the grounds of the Royal Hospital.

"Just refuelling!" called out Elsie.

The old soldier shook his

head. "Ruddy strange sort of tank."

"Yes, it doubles up as a lawnmower," said Dotty.

Just as the pair thought they might have got away with it, the inevitable happened. The animal laid a mammoth poop.

PPPFFFT!

THUD!

The prehistoric poop plopped on to the snow. It was mammoth both in origin and size, large and brown and steaming.

"Just testing the brand-new weaponry," explained Elsie.

"It's a stink bomb," added Dotty.

"Don't worry!" began Elsie. "It's not explosive!" Then she added under her breath, "I think."

"Well, you can't leave it there on the lawn!" roared the sergeant major.

"What do you want us to do with it?" asked Elsie.

"Put it back in the chute."

The pair looked at the back end of the mammoth.

"I'm not sure that's going to work," said Dotty.

"I'd say it's more of an exit than an entrance."

"Well, pick it up, then!" he ordered.

"Me?" asked Dotty. She'd been a cleaning lady for forty years and had dealt with all kinds of unspeakable mess, but this was beyond beyond.

"Yes, you," said Elsie.

The lady gave the little girl a stern look.

"Don't dilly-dally, woman. Get on with it!" bellowed the sergeant major.

Reluctantly, Dotty bent down. Holding her nose as far away from the hot steaming pile as possible, the lady scooped it up in her hands. She stood up and held it away from her as far as her arms would allow.

"At last!" called out the sergeant major.

The three unlikely friends moved on. The little girl couldn't help but smile, which made the lady fume.

"Would you care to swap?" asked Dotty, already knowing the answer.

"I'm fine, thank you," said Elsie, leading the mammoth across the courtyard. She noticed an unusually short old soldier looking out at them from a tall window. He was smiling, waving and blowing

kisses in the most extravagant manner.

"TITCH!" exclaimed Dotty.

Chapter 43

A GRAVE MISTAKE

"It just looks like a hairy elephant to me," remarked Titch in his musical Welsh accent.

Elsie was pleased to finally meet this man she'd heard so much about. He was indeed short. Not even taller than her. In fact, Dotty was as wide as he was tall. There was no denying that they made an unusual match. However, all that mattered was that the pair glowed in each other's presence.

The animal was drinking water from a toilet stall in the Royal Hospital, her trunk stuck down the U-bend.

"Well, she's not a hairy elephant!" replied Elsie haughtily. **"She's a woolly mammoth."**

"I've never heard of such a thing!" scoffed Titch.

"Well, that doesn't mean it doesn't exist! It's a prehistoric creature."

"I'm prehistoric myself, and I don't remember seeing those as a boy in the Welsh valleys."

"Well, that's because woolly mammoths died out thousands of years ago."

"And you just brought her back to life, did you?" said the man with a chuckle.

"Yes," replied Elsie. "Actually, we did!"

This stopped the old soldier in his tracks. He looked at Dotty for confirmation. The lady nodded her head.

"Well, what the ruddy hell is she doing here?" he demanded.

"I was rather hoping you might help us hide her!" replied Dotty.

"Me?"

"Yes."

"Here?"

"Yes."

"A great big furry elephant?"

"Well, no." Elsie jumped in to correct him. "She's a woolly mammoth."

"How long for?" he asked.

"They live for fifty years or more."

"FIFTY?"

"Yes. This is just a baby one."

"How big do they grow?"

"To about the size of a house."

"A house?"

Just then there was the sound of a flush in the stall next door.

SPLISH!

An impossibly old man shuffled out, wearing a nightshirt with a military cap, and leaning on a cane. The three looked at one another in panic. They'd had no idea the man had been in there the whole time.

"Morning, Colonel," said Titch.

"I'd leave that a minute if I were you," muttered the colonel, wafting the air and actually making the smell worse, not better. Despite the stink, the three smiled back at him, but said nothing, hoping he might shuffle on.

He didn't.

The colonel spotted the rear end of the mammoth sticking out of the stall next to his. He took a moment to admire it, before commenting. "My word, that's quite a remarkable large, furry bottom. New boy, is he?"

"It's a pet," replied Titch.

"A pet?"

"Yes! Now I would hate for you to miss your breakfast, Colonel. Let me help you to the dining hall."

The private took the colonel by the arm, but the old man was having none of it.

"You can't keep a pet in the Royal Hospital, Private! It is against regulations!"

"It won't be here for long," replied Titch, shooting a look at Dotty.

"No more than fifty years, Colonel, sir," chipped in the lady.

Elsie shook her head in disbelief at Dotty's stupidity.

"FIFTY YEARS!" spluttered the colonel. "What kind of animal is this thing, anyway?"

"She's a woolly mammoth," replied Elsie.

"A what?" asked the man.

"It's like a hairy elephant," added Dotty.

"We can't have a hairy elephant in here!" shouted the man. "Whatever is this country coming to? Get the blasted beast out!" With that, he whacked the mammoth's bottom with his stick.

THWACK!

This would prove to be a grave mistake.

Chapter 44

❖

RIGHT UP
MY WHATSIT

"**N**O!" shouted Elsie. "**HOOO!**" cried the animal. She began bucking from side to side.

CRUNCH!

The wooden partitions between the toilets splintered into pieces as the mammoth struggled to get out. When she lurched backwards, the colonel gave her another whack with his cane.

"**TAKE THAT,** YOU HAIRY-BOTTOMED BEAST!"

THWACK!

"**STOP!**" cried Elsie. She lurched at the colonel, and held on to his arm to stop him striking her friend again.

"Get your filthy hands off me, girl!"

The mammoth was trying to turn herself round in the cramped toilet. Her tusks bashed into the toilet bowl...

CRASH!

...smashing it to pieces.

SPLURT!

Water began gushing everywhere, soaking everybody and everything.

"URGH!" cried the colonel.

"Oh dearie me. More mess for me to clean up!" remarked Dotty, never one to leave her job far behind.

"I'm going to be in big trouble with Matron," said

Titch, desperately trying to sit on all the toilets at once to stop water spraying across the ceiling. All he achieved was an incredibly wet bottom.

"Ooh!" he screamed as he was propelled into the air. "The water's going right up my whatsit!"

Eventually, the mammoth managed to turn herself round, and ripped the cane out of the man's hands with her trunk. With all her might, she hurled the cane across the room.

W H I Z Z !

It hit the window…

BANG!

…shattering it.

CRACK!

"Oh, cripes! Not another breakage," muttered the lady.

The water level in the room was rising rapidly. All four humans and the mammoth were soon knee-deep in it.

With all the noise, it was only a matter of time before someone came thumping on the door.

THUD!
THUD!
THUD!

"What in heaven's name is happening in there?" came a female voice.

"Matron!" hissed Titch, a flash of panic in his eyes. Then he raised his voice. "It's all right, Matron. Everything is under control. Just a minor problem with the flush."

The colonel, who had only come in for a quiet morning poo, was having no more of this nonsense.

"**Matron!** They've got some great hairy elephant in here!"

"Seeing things again, Colonel?" she called out.

"See for yourself, woman!" he called back.

Matron pushed open the door. A ten-thousand-year-old woolly mammoth was staring back at her. But before she had time to scream a rush of water swept her off her feet...

WHOOSH!

...and carried her down the corridor at speed.

The other five all popped their heads round the door to watch her go.

"At least that floor is getting a good clean," remarked Dotty to herself.

Chapter 45

A LIDOLLOP

Fortunately, there were many fantastic hiding places in the Royal Hospital. With Matron flushed away, Titch led Elsie, Dotty and Woolly down to the food-storage room, and slammed the door behind them.

"It's nice and chilly in here," said Titch. "I'm sure your furry friend will feel right at home."

The mammoth did. Elsie did too, for this was where all the food for the elderly soldiers was kept. The old boys obviously ate well as there were giant jars of sweets, and tins of all sorts of goodies, like jam, honey and treacle. To a girl who had lived her entire life under the shadow of hunger, the smell of the food was like the sweetest perfume.

"I'm starving," said Elsie. "Please may I have a tiny bit of jam?"

The little girl's eyes widened, and her lip quivered. How could the grown-ups possibly say no?

"A little dollop can't hurt, can it?" said Dotty.

"No," agreed Titch. "No one would miss a dollop."

"Strawberry or raspberry?" asked Dotty.

"I've never had either," replied the girl. "What's nicer?"

"Raspberry, I think."

"**Raspberry** it is, then!"

Titch reached up, and took down a jar of raspberry jam. Slowly, he unscrewed the lid as the little girl licked her lips. However, before Elsie could dip her finger in, a huge furry trunk snaked around and slurped up the lot.

SLURP!

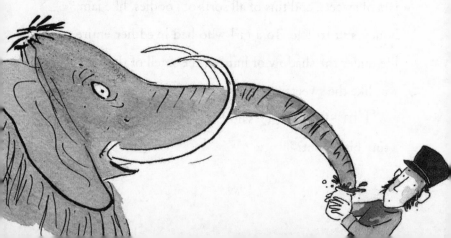

"What the…?" exclaimed Elsie.

"Bad manmoth!" chided Dotty, slapping Woolly's trunk away.

WHACK!

The mammoth didn't even react. She was too busy being in a state of bliss at having tasted jam for the first time.

"Maybe I should try some **strawberry,** then?" said Elsie.

But as Titch unscrewed the lid the mammoth's trunk snaked its way around and slurped up every last bit.

SLURP!

"WHAT?" exclaimed Elsie.

"BAD MANMOTH!" yelled Dotty.

"Not too loud!" hissed Titch.

"Well, she's being very naughty!"

"I know. But, if I know Matron, she'll have all the soldiers up out of their beds looking for that thing."

"She's not a thing," said Elsie. "She's a mammoth."

"Mammoth thing, then. I don't know!"

RUMBLE!

"What was that?" asked Elsie.

"Thunder?" guessed Dotty.

RUMBLE!

"There it is again!" exclaimed the girl.

"Is it the pipes?" wondered Titch.

RUMBLE!

"It is the pipes!" said Elsie. "Woolly's pipes! Listen!"

All three fell silent.

RUMBLE!

"It must be the jam," said Dotty, "not agreeing with her tum-tum. Don't let her have any more."

"I won't," replied the girl. "But I am absolutely starving. You hold her trunk while I have a tiny bit of treacle."

The treacle was in a huge tin the size of a bucket. Titch shook his head and lifted it down towards the girl as Dotty blocked the animal's view with her body, and held on tightly to its trunk. Excitedly, Elsie prised the lid off. Immediately, the sugary aroma whispered its way up her nostrils. It was so sweet that for a moment the girl felt as if she were floating. She dipped her finger in, and it felt as smooth as silk.

Just as she was about to scoop out a large dollop of treacle, she was shoved against the shelves, causing all the tins and jars to come crashing to the floor.

BANG!

CRASH!

WALLOP!

The mammoth had surged forward to slurp up every last bit of the sweet-smelling gloop. Dotty was holding on to the animal's trunk, so was shoved into Titch, who was shoved into Elsie. Now there was a cloud of sugar and flour and tea whirling around the room, causing the three non-mammoths to cough and splutter. In amongst the chaos, the mammoth's trunk searched out every last morsel of food that had been splattered on the walls, floor or ceiling – or, indeed, was still floating through the air.

The more they all tried to stop Woolly from devouring everything in sight, the faster she ate.

RUMBLE!
GURGLE!
FUZZLE!

"Oh no, listen to her tummy again!" said Dotty.

"I think we're heading for an explosion," predicted Titch.

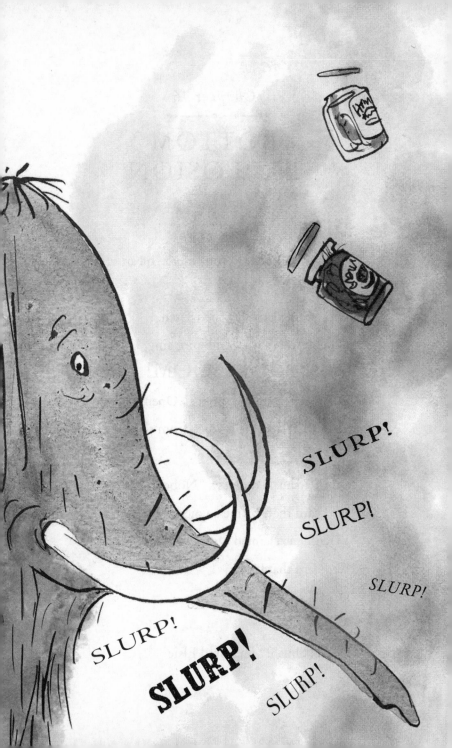

Chapter 46

❖

BOTTOM
EXPLOSION

The girl gulped. "You don't mean a bottom explosion?" she asked.

"I do, young lady," replied Titch.

Suddenly, there was loud knocking.

BOOM! BOOM! BOOM!

"This is the military police! Open up! We know you're in there!" came a voice from the other side of the door.

"Shush!" shushed Dotty. "Nobody say a word!"

"We heard that," came a voice.

"YIKES!" exclaimed Dotty.

"We heard that too!"

"Darn!"

"And that."

"Dotty! Shush!" implored Elsie.

"We heard that as well."

"It wasn't me that time!" called back Dotty.

GRUMBLE! TRIZZLE! DURGLE!

"I fear a bottom explosion is coming," said the little old soldier, "at a terrifying speed!"

BOOM! BOOM! BOOM!

"Open this door at once!"

"Well, why don't we?" said Elsie with a smirk.

"You don't mean use its rear end as a cannon?" asked the little soldier.

"Exactly!" replied the girl. "Open the door and fire at will!"

"Just coming, officers!" called out Dotty, as she squeezed past the mammoth to get to the door.

"QUICKLY, MADAM, OR WE WILL BE FORCED TO BREAK THIS DOOR DOWN!"

"Patience is a virtue!" she called back.

TUZZER! GROOBLE! FUJOOZZLE!

"By the sound of Woolly, she's ready to blow!" said Elsie.

Dotty put her hand on the key, and began to turn it in the lock.

"Just a jiffy, officers!"

CLICK! went the key.

"The door is unlocked!" Dotty called out.

CROOMADOOB! MUNTYMUNTY! BOODADOOZLE!

The handle turned and slowly the door opened.

The three shared a mischievous look as the mammoth straightened her back and lifted her tail.

"FIRE!" shouted Titch.

Fire the creature did.

GGGRRRUUURRR!

The noise of Woolly's bottom burping sounded just like a bear growling.

It fired all over the military policemen, covering them from head to toe in hot, sticky mammoth poop. The force of the bottom blast was so strong it knocked them off their feet. The poor men were completely disorientated, as their eyes and noses were covered in the stuff.

"Let's make a run for it!" said Elsie.

"CHARGE!" cried Titch.

The three guided the animal back out of the larder, and began leading her down the corridor.

"You bring up the rear, Dotty!" ordered the old soldier.

"Not on your nelly!" snapped the lady. "I don't trust that area one bit!"

"Where are we going?" asked Elsie.

"Away from that awful smell!" replied Titch as they hurried along the corridor and up the stairs to his ward.

. -→ * ←- .

Chapter 47

A NEW COMRADE

"This is where I sleep!" announced Titch, as he opened the door to his ward.

"We should have hidden Woolly in here in the first place," muttered Elsie.

"I think he shares it with other people," replied Dotty.

"Well, I'm sure we could have told a few old soldiers to keep their traps shut."

The door opened to reveal not a few, but twenty old soldiers, all poking their heads out of their berths.

"Oops!" said Elsie.

Slowly, Titch led the woolly mammoth into the ward by the tusk. He coughed and cleared his throat.

"Good morning, gentlemen. Gentlemen! If I could

have your attention, please. I would like to introduce you to a new comrade."

The old soldiers put on their spectacles, attached any wooden arms and legs, or sidled into wheelchairs. Slowly, they approached the magnificent beast.

"What in God's name is it, Titch?" piped up one.

"Does it bite, Private?" asked another.

"Is this what we're having for breakfast?" said a third, who had a long white beard that made him look like a military Father Christmas.

Elsie stepped forward. "No. This is my friend, Woolly."

"Good Lord! A female in the Royal Hospital!" remarked one old soldier.

"And another!" said another.

"The hairy elephant thingummy can stay! But they need to go!" exclaimed a third.

"HOO!" Woolly seemed to hoot in agreement.

"Three females in the Royal Hospital!" thundered another old soldier. "This is a disgrace!"

"It's worse than the Boer War!"

"This place will have to be closed down!"

"It's a scandal of **EPIC PROPORTIONS!**"

Titch raised his voice to shout over them. "Let's have some hush, men! Wait until you hear the girl's story. Elsie…"

The girl smiled, and cleared her throat.

As she told the story so far, the old soldiers were rapt. They had heard stories of **incredible bravery and derring-do**, but this tall tale topped them all.

Elsie ended with a plea. "Gentlemen! Will you help Woolly?"

"I'm in!" came one voice.

"I am too!" came another.

"Me too."

"And me."

"And me!" said another and another and another, until all but one soldier had raised his hand. All eyes turned to the one who hadn't.

"Sorry, what was the question again?" asked the one who looked like Father Christmas.

"That's the brigadier," said Titch. "He forgets

things. We'll take that as a yes."

"Who forgets what?" asked the brigadier.

The mammoth lolloped over to the window at the far end of the long ward and looked out. Elsie trailed after her friend, before following her gaze over the rooftops of London. Woolly lifted her trunk and pressed it against the windowpane, as if longing for something way out of reach. Elsie stroked the mammoth's trunk, then lifted one of her big furry ears and whispered into it.

"What are you looking at, my friend?" she whispered. "If only you could tell me."

"HOO!"

Chapter 48

NORTH, NORTH, NORTH

Dotty ambled down the ward to join the pair. "Do you think we could teach Woolly to talk?"

"Talk?"

"Yep. Then she could tell us what she was looking at."

"But how would we teach her to talk?"

"That would be the tricky bit," replied Dotty, looking lost in thought. "Maybe we could teach her one **HOO** for yes, and two **HOOS** for no, and three **HOOS** for maybe? Then list all the places in the world and see what she says?"

Elsie didn't want to hurt the lady's feelings. "It's a great idea, Dotty. It just might take a while to go through every single place in the world."

She turned round to address the old soldiers.

"Does anyone have a **compass**?" she asked.

"Admiral, you're never without yours!" said Titch.

"That's right, Private!" replied the admiral. He began patting his pyjama pockets. "Now, where did I put the blasted thing?"

"It's round your neck!" said Titch.

The admiral found it on the end of a chain. "It's round my neck! Why didn't you tell me?" He took it off and limped over to the girl.

DUFF! DUFF! DUFF!

Elsie noticed one of his legs was wooden.

"My leg, before you ask, was bitten off by a shark. Cheeky blighter did me a favour, really – I had gangrene anyway, so the leg had turned green. Didn't have to have it sawn off. Shark died of food poisoning. Rum old business."

The admiral passed the compass to Elsie.

"There we are, young lady. We haven't been introduced. I am the admiral. The only naval man in here."

"He was thrown out of the old sailors' home for drunkenness," remarked Titch.

"That night I'd only drunk seven bottles of rum, Private!" thundered the admiral. "It takes at least nine to get me drunk!"

A cloud of rum-smelling breath sailed right up Elsie's nose. Her eyes watered, and she sneezed. It was so strong that for a moment she herself felt drunk.

"Thank you, Admiral," replied the girl. Elsie held the compass flat in her hand. The black arrow was pointing exactly the way the mammoth was pointing too.

"NORTH!" exclaimed Elsie.

"HOO!" went the mammoth.

"See, she does talk!" added Dotty. "Every time, Woolly has been pining to go north."

"HOO!"

"She's talking again," remarked Dotty.

"So, Admiral, tell me this…" said Elsie.

"Yes, young lady?" replied the old man, with a smile.

"What is the absolute furthest north you can go?"

The admiral guided the girl over to his bedside.

"Behold my globe, child!"

Beside his bed stood a magnificent orb with a map of the world on it. "This came from my ship."

"Before it sank," chipped in Titch.

"That's quite enough of that, Private. I adore gazing at my globe. It reminds me of my glory days, all those adventures on the high seas! Look, young lady, we are here in London."

He indicated the spot on the globe. "Pop your finger there."

The girl did so.

"Now trace your finger north, north, north."

As Elsie moved her finger up, the admiral read out the places. "Scotland, Orkney Islands, Iceland, Greenland, the Arctic, the North Pole. You can't get any more north than that."

"The North Pole!" said Elsie. "Is it cold?"

The soldiers couldn't help but laugh.

"It's SO cold, young lady," began the admiral, "that the sea is **permanently frozen**. There is no land, just a huge expanse of ice."

"ICE!" she exclaimed. "Perfect for a creature from the Ice Age. That's where we must take Woolly! To the North Pole!"

"HOO!" agreed Woolly.

Elsie lifted her arms in a triumphant show of leadership. She looked around the ward. Every single old soldier stared back at her, mouth open in shock.

Chapter 49

❖

AUDACIOUS

"But how would we get to that there the North Pole?" asked Titch.

"We would sail, soldier!" announced the admiral. "This is a job for the navy."

"But surely you'll need the army for ground support, sir," replied Titch.

"You may be right there, Private. This is a job for both divisions of Her Majesty's armed forces. A joint navy and, to a lesser extent, army mission."

"Hang on, hang on, hang on!" interrupted Dotty.

"What is it, woman?" thundered the admiral.

"Don't you need a boat?"

There were murmurs from the soldiers.

"She has a point."

"She's not as daft as she looks."

"I think we're missing a chess piece."

"Yes," agreed the admiral. "If you're sailing, it's always best to make sure you have a boat, otherwise there's a strong chance you will get decidedly wet. Now, where are we going to get a boat from?"

All the old men became lost in thought, but Elsie began imagining a theft so audacious it would make the **Sticky Fingers Gang** seem like nuns.

"I know where there's a boat you can pinch!" she announced.

All eyes turned to her. There were some mocking mumbles from the old men.

"She's a mere child."

312

"The girl knows nothing about boats."

"This tea tastes of coffee. It is coffee!"

The admiral limped over to the girl, his wooden leg thump-thump-thumping on the floor.

DUFF! DUFF! DUFF!

"Pray tell us, young lady," he began grandly, "where is this boat you speak of?"

The girl consulted the compass to see which was east, then found a window facing in that direction.

"It's out there!" replied Elsie smugly, pointing down towards the River Thames.

The old man hurried over to the window as fast as his leg would carry him.

DUFF! DUFF! DUFF!

All the old soldiers followed. They gathered behind the admiral, eager to see where the girl was pointing.

"There!" said the girl. "YOU CAN STEAL HMS VICTORY."

· ⇁ ✳ ↼ ·

Chapter 50

RELIC

The magnificent old sailing ship was now a museum piece and, to celebrate the coming of the new century, had been moved from Portsmouth and moored on the Thames.

"HMS *Victory*?" announced the admiral, before hooting with laughter. "HO! HO! HO!"

"*HA! HA! HA!*" chimed in the men.

Elsie was so annoyed she crossed her arms and gave them all a stern look.

"What's so funny?" she demanded.

"My dear child," began the admiral, "HMS *Victory* was Lord Nelson's flagship in the Battle of Trafalgar all the way back in 1805. She's over a hundred years old! She's a relic!"

"So are you!" snapped back the girl. "But you can still sail, can't you?"

The admiral's face soured, but there was a hint of grudging respect in his voice. "Feisty one, aren't you?"

"I have been told so, yes."

"Mmm, well, it would be quite an honour to follow in Lord Nelson's footsteps," mused the admiral. "Do you know what, men? I think this young lady might be on to something!"

Elsie beamed with pride.

"With respect, sir," interrupted Titch, "the military police may have been splattered with mammoth poop, but they will soon be on to us. We need to make a plan, and fast."

"Yes," announced the girl. "Everyone listen to me!"

The old soldiers were taken aback. Never in their long lives had they taken orders from a little girl, let alone an unwashed urchin like Elsie.

"Well, young lady," announced the admiral, "we would all dearly love to know your plan."

There were murmurs from the men.

"Yes, we would."

"A girl with a plan, whatever next?"

"Do you think we'll get a bath today?"

"We don't have much time." Elsie raised her voice.

"So, gentlemen, please listen."

The admiral sailed in. "You heard what the young lady said, men. We don't have much time, so everyone needs to stop talking and listen."

"Yes!" replied Elsie. "That includes you, Admiral."

There were snickers of laughter from the men.

"HEE! HEE! HEE!"

Nobody had ever spoken to the admiral like that, and the man's face was glowing the colour of the Chelsea Pensioners' scarlet coats.

"**Right!**" began the girl. "We need two divisions. The *FIRST* men need to make their way along the Thames to where HMS *Victory* is moored, and steal her. Then sail her down here to the hospital. We're just a stone's throw away from the river. The *SECOND* division needs to raid the larder, and gather as many provisions as possible. Admiral?"

"Yes, sir! I mean, madam. I mean, miss," spluttered the old sailor.

"How long will it take us to sail to the North Pole?"

The admiral limped over to his globe...

DUFF! DUFF! DUFF!

...and traced his finger along the route. "Down the Thames, into the English Channel. North Sea. Norwegian Sea. Greenland Sea. Arctic Ocean, and boom! We're there. No more than three or four weeks."

"What if I need the loo?" asked Dotty.

"You go over the side like a sailor, madam!" replied the admiral. "It's the only way to go!"

"He still plops out of the window," remarked Titch.

"It's refreshing!"

"Not for anyone standing below."

"Three to four weeks," began Elsie. "We'll need a lot of food. Not least for this one!" she added, stroking her prehistoric friend.

"HOO!" agreed Woolly.

"It's going to be very nippy up there at the North Pole," said Dotty.

"Good point, Dotty! So we'll need all the warm clothes you can get hold of."

The admiral put up his hand.

"Yes, Admiral?" asked Elsie.

"Please can I be in charge of the ship?" he asked meekly.

"Yes, of course you can, Admiral."

"Thank you! Thank you! Thank you! Me in charge of HMS *Victory*. This is a dream come true!"

"You pick ten men, and bring back the *Victory*."

"Right," began the admiral. "This is a dangerous mission. It could even be fatal. I need ten good men and true."

All the old soldiers puffed out their chests, and put on their most noble expressions, dying to be picked.

Chapter 51

ONE LONELY MEDAL

The admiral selected his crack team. Ten men threw their scarlet coats and black trousers on over their pyjamas, and, as their medals clinked together, they put on their tricorne hats. Elsie noticed that, unlike all the other soldiers, Titch just had the one lonely medal.

"Why has Titch only got one medal?" she whispered to Dotty.

"Ooh, don't ask!" she replied. "It's a sore point. They all tease him for it."

"Fall in!" roared the admiral.

The old soldiers organised themselves into a line. They may all have been battered by age and ill health, but they stood to attention with the same pride as the first day they signed up. Between them, they had served in the Crimean War against the Russians, battled their way across India and fought the Zulu warriors in Africa. Now, they were ready for the adventure of their lives.

The admiral approached the mammoth, and saluted her.

"We won't let you down, ma'am mammoth," he said.

"HOO!" replied Woolly, lifting her trunk as if saluting back.

"Now, men, quick march!"

With that, he led his men out of the ward.

"I need to stay here and look after Woolly," said Elsie. "You, Titch, gather up all the food you can lay your hands on. There must be something Woolly didn't eat."

"HOO!"

"I'll do my best, Elsie," replied the private.

"Thank you, Titch. And, Dotty, grab every last hat, glove and coat in here. Load them on to the ship, and then both of you come back to fetch us."

"Right you are!" Titch replied.

There were murmurs from the old soldiers.

"Not sure about Titch being put in charge."

"He's only a private!"

"Man's only got the one medal!"

"And that he got for service!"

"He's no hero!"

"This egg is repeating on me!"

Dotty put a comforting hand on her beloved's shoulder. "Don't take any notice."

"I'll show you, boys!" said Titch. "Now come on, follow me!"

With that, he led his comrades and Dotty across the ward, and left Elsie alone with her woolly friend.

"Lock this door," ordered Titch as he reached it.

"Good thought!" replied the girl.

"I'll knock twice. Then you'll know it's safe to open it."

"Understood."

"Two fast knocks or two slow knocks?" asked Dotty.

"It doesn't matter, my love!" snapped the soldier. "Just two knocks! KNOCK! KNOCK! I'll meet you back here as soon as we're ready to set sail."

Elsie rushed over to the door, and locked it behind them.

CLICK!

Then she crossed the ward to join Woolly. The girl put her arms round her.

"Don't worry, Woolly," she said. "We're going to get you home."

"HOO!" Woolly nodded her head.

Then the animal yawned, and Elsie did too. Woolly folded down on to her knees, and rolled over on to her side before letting out a long, slow sigh.

"HOOOOOOO!"

Elsie lay down next to her friend, her back nestling up against the animal's belly. The mammoth curled her trunk round the girl and held her tight. This was a world away from the cold tin bath Elsie normally slept in. Together they closed their eyes.

"Goodnight, Woolly."

"HOO."

The pair breathed in and out in time with each other, and soon both had fallen asleep. Little did they know that someone was peering in at them through the window.

.➤*✦*◄.

Chapter 52

RAMPAGE

O utside the window to the ward, the top of a ladder had appeared. And at the top of the ladder a pair of beady eyes, a long nose and a tiny moustache had appeared. It was Commissioner Barker. He spied the pair sleeping, and signalled to the officers below to keep quiet.

"WHAT?" one called up loudly from the ground.

"A finger on the lips means *be quiet*," he hissed back.

"RIGHTY-HO!" the constable on the ground shouted up.

"SHUSH!"

"GOT IT!"

As the snow swirled around him, Commissioner

Barker slid down the ladder, his feet landing with a crunch in the snow.

KRUNDLE!

"This time, we're not going to let them get away."

THUD!

THUD!

The noise woke up Elsie and Woolly with a start. The girl was sure she'd heard two knocks. But they were much louder than she'd anticipated.

She wanted to call out for Dotty, but her throat tightened in fear, and she couldn't make a sound.

THUD!

Another knock. Something wasn't right. It was very wrong. Elsie moved backwards, and felt Woolly wrap her trunk protectively round her.

"HOO!" she whimpered.

THUD!

This time the door buckled.

THUD!

Shards of wood went flying.

THUD!

328

BOOM!

The doors smashed off their hinges and fell to the floor.

DOOF! DOOF!

Framed in the doorway was Commissioner Barker, flanked by a dozen of his men holding a battering ram.

"Are you going to come quietly?" he bellowed.

"HOO!" roared the mammoth.

The sound gave Elsie strength.

"No! We're going to come really noisily!"

With that, she clambered on to the animal's back, and gave her a whack on her side.

"CHARGE!" shouted Elsie.

Woolly knew exactly what to do, and galloped towards the men.

"Hold the line!" ordered Barker.

The policemen all looked at one another nervously as they linked arms.

"HOLD THE LINE!"

The policemen gripped one another tight.

"HOLD THE LINE!"

Barker was the first to disobey his own order. He broke away from his men and leaped out of the way. His men followed suit, leaving Woolly and Elsie free to escape down the corridor.

"COWARDS!" shouted Barker. "FOOLS!"

Of course, the policemen were the exact opposite of fools, sensibly having no desire to be trampled to death by a prehistoric creature.

Seeing the flight of descending stairs ahead, the mammoth came to an abrupt halt.

"**WHOA!**" cried Elsie, as the force of the sudden stop hurled her through the air.

W H I Z Z !

She landed on her bottom with a THUD on the top step…

DRUMPH!

…before sliding down the remaining steps at speed.

BONK!

BONK!

BONK!

Woolly looked on with interest. Maybe this was the best way to go down stairs. She sat on her bottom and slid down too.

BONK!

BONK!

BONK!

"HOO! HOO! HOO!"

These were much bigger

BONKS. After all, the

mammoth had an infinitely larger bottom. But, going by the little yelps she let out as her bottom hit each step, she seemed to enjoy it.

Soon the pair were lying in a crumpled heap at the bottom of the stairs.

Seeing the policemen arriving at the top, Elsie pulled Woolly along by her trunk.

"HOO!" cried the animal.

Spotting an open doorway, they raced in. It was a huge, grand dining room with chandeliers hanging from the ceiling and wooden panels on the walls. Table upon table was laid out neatly for breakfast. Table upon table was upturned as the mammoth charged through the room.

"HOO!"

CRASH!

BANG!

WALLOP!

A gaggle of cooks dashed out from a kitchen door to see what the rumpus was all about.

"WHAT IS THE MEANING OF THIS?" demanded one.

As soon as they saw it was a mammoth rampaging through the dining hall, they dashed back into the kitchen.

"SORRY TO DISTURB YOU! PLEASE CARRY ON!"

The policemen arrived at the doors.

"THE MONSTER IS THE PROPERTY OF HER MAJESTY THE QUEEN!" shouted Barker. "WE HAVE OUR ORDERS TO RETURN IT! ALIVE OR PREFERABLY DEAD!"

Immediately, Elsie leaped on to her friend's back, so they couldn't shoot, and raced towards the set of tall doors at the far end of the room. However, those doors swung open to reveal Matron, and a rather pooey-looking group of military policemen holding rifles.

"We have you trapped!" bawled Matron. "Now give yourselves up!"

"NEVER!" shouted the girl.

The military policemen lifted their rifles. The animal reared up on her hind legs and roared a huge roar.

"HOOO!"

Elsie's head clinked against the bottom of a chandelier. Thinking fast, she grabbed hold of it and swung backwards before launching herself at the doorway. She flew through the air and hit Matron and the military policemen like a bowling ball striking some skittles…

BASH!

…sending them flying.

"ARGH!"

THUD

THUD

THUD!

They rolled out of the way as the mammoth thundered past. Elsie sprang to her feet, and leaped back on to Woolly as she escaped through the door.

Chapter 53

◆

DANGER EVERYWHERE

The plan was unravelling fast. Now there was no way Elsie and Woolly could wait for HMS *Victory* to reach the Royal Hospital. Danger was everywhere. They had to keep moving. The pair fled through the doors, past the columns and the statue of the hospital's much-loved founder, Charles II, and across the lawn that led down to the Thames. The river was frozen over. Would the ice take the weight of a two-ton mammoth? With policemen chasing them across the snow with rifles, there was only one way to find out.

BANG! BANG! BANG!

Shots rang out. Birds in the trees took to the sky in fear. Elsie ducked her head, and dug her heels into the animal's sides to make her gallop faster.

"HOO!"

Woolly charged across the snow and leaped off the riverbank, landing hard on the ice.

THUD!

Fortunately, the ice didn't crack, but it was slippery from all the ice skaters. The mammoth's legs slid out from under her, and she went spinning across the ice.

"HOOO!"

"NOOO!" screamed Elsie.

They'd hit the ice so fast there was no stopping them. Round and round they whirled, the mammoth's legs splayed out like a starfish.

WHIZZ!

Woolly ploughed through some early-morning ice skaters, who were sent spinning across the ice as if they were part of some mass dance spectacular.

"ARGH!" they cried.

"SORRY!" called out Elsie, not that the apology seemed to help at all. Up ahead was a small rowing boat that must have become stuck in the ice. They were speeding right towards it.

W H I Z Z !

The girl closed her eyes.

BOOM!

The boat smashed into pieces. Wood exploded across the ice. The force of the blow caused Elsie to become separated from her friend.

"NOOO!"

They each came to a stop on opposite banks of the river. Battered and bruised, the girl rose unsteadily to her feet. She looked across the ice. The poor mammoth was having a much more difficult time of it. Every time it looked like she was back on four legs, one would slip from under her, and her belly would flop down on the ice.

DOOF!

"HOO!"

On her bare feet, Elsie skated
over to help her friend. When
she saw one of Woolly's legs
sliding down, she would lean
all her weight against it to
push it up. But her little frame
was no match for the mammoth's,
and down they would both go.

DOOF!

"HOO!"

Finally, Elsie managed to skate round the mammoth,
pushing each leg in turn, making sure they were all
upright. In the distance, she could see their pursuers
gathering on the riverbanks.

"Come on!" she ordered, but, as soon as she had
led the mammoth one step forward, she landed flat on
her belly again.

BOSH!

Elsie looked across the frozen Thames. There were

planks of wood from the boat they had destroyed scattered across the ice. These planks were long and thin, and looked a little like the things she'd seen posh folk attach to the bottoms of their shoes to race down a snow-topped Primrose Hill last winter.

Skis!

As fast as she could, Elsie skated over to them. She picked up two of the planks and a length of rope that must have been lying in the rowing boat, before skating back to her friend. Elsie laid them down in front of the mammoth. Then she skated round the back, encouraging Woolly up by pushing on her bottom.

"HOO!"

An exhausted Woolly soon got the message, and stepped forward on to the "skis".

In the distance, Barker and his men took to the ice, closely followed by Matron and the military

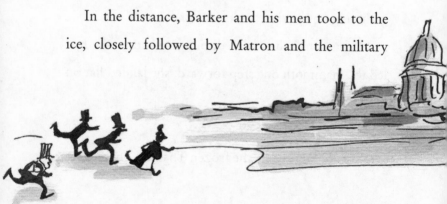

policemen. As quickly as she could, Elsie picked up the rope and held it out in front of the mammoth's mouth. Woolly bit into it.

"Clever girl," whispered Elsie.

"HOO!"

With all her might, Elsie pulled on the rope.

The mammoth inched forward.

Darn!

This wasn't going to work.

Darn and blast!

Elsie tried again, and really yanked this time. This created some momentum. Soon the impossible was happening.

A real-life mammoth was skiing across a frozen River Thames!

WHOOSH! WHOOSH! WHOOSH! went the skis on the ice.

"HOO!" called out Woolly joyfully, loving the feeling of speed, her fur blowing in the cold breeze!

They passed by a man roasting chestnuts on the snow.

"Lovely morning!" remarked Elsie as they slid by.

Even the orphans back at WORMLY HALL wouldn't believe this! The man stared open-mouthed in shock as the prehistoric animal let out another excited…

"HOOOOOOOOOOOOOOOOOOOO!"

· ➛ ✳ ↢ ·

Chapter 54

HMS *VICTORY*

Ahead in the distance, emerging out of the fog like a ghost ship, was HMS *Victory*.

The three masts reaching up to the sky.

The tall, square stern with dozens of windows.

The magnificent crest at the top.

At the bottom, written in big proud strokes, were the letters V I C T O R Y. Elsie couldn't read, but she knew what they spelled. HMS *Victory* was the most famous ship in all the kingdom, if not the entire world.

As she and Woolly skied nearer, she could see the admiral and his men hoisting the topsail. Closer still, she could make out Dotty, Titch and their team loading boxes on to the ship. The girl couldn't help but smile. They were going to make it.

RAT TAT TAT TAT TAT!

It was the sound of a machine gun from up above! They were being attacked from the skies!

Shots scattered across the ice, narrowly missing the pair.

The shock caused Elsie to stumble. As she tumbled, so did Woolly. They hit the ice hard.

BOOF! BOOF!

"AH!" screamed Elsie in pain.

"HOO!" cried the mammoth.

Elsie looked up. Through the fog, she spotted something the size of a blue whale floating in the sky. It was so large it was blotting out the sun.

It was a Zeppelin,* one of the huge state-of-the-art German airships.

In the gondola underneath, a woman with a distinctive pith helmet on her head and a murderous look on her face was positioned behind a machine gun.

It was Lady Buckshot, the big-game hunter. You could smell that foul cigar smoke for miles around.

RAT TAT TAT TAT TAT!

Another hail of bullets rained down. They went straight through the ice, blasting holes in it.

PWANG! PWANG! PWANG!

Freezing-cold river water flooded on to the ice. Slowly but surely, Elsie, who was still lying down, felt it trickle down her neck and up her sleeves. She looked over to her friend.

Woolly was sinking. And fast.

"HOOO!"

Named after its pioneer, Count Ferdinand von Zeppelin. A Zeppelin consisted of a gondola under a huge envelope of hydrogen.

RAT TAT TAT TAT TAT!

More bullets. More holes. More cracks. More water. More danger.

"HOOOO!" yelled the animal in fear.

Elsie held on to her friend's trunk.

"It's going to be all right, Woolly. I'm going to get us out of this. I promise."

RAT TAT TAT TAT TAT!

"HOOOOO!?"

The ice beneath them exploded into pieces.

KABOOM!

The pair were plunged deep into the icy water.

"NOOOOO!" screamed the girl as she disappeared into the depths.

· ⚹ ·

Chapter 55

BLACK SILENCE

E verything went dark.

All Elsie could see was black.

All she could hear was silence.

All the girl could feel was a deathly chill.

At first, she didn't know what was up and what was down.

Where was Woolly?

In all the chaos and confusion, she had lost sight and sound and touch of her friend. Immediately, the cruel current of the Thames pulled her far away from the hole she had fallen through. As much as Elsie tried to paddle back to it, that proved impossible. She was being swept further and further away. In desperation, she thumped on the underside of the ice, trying to bash her way through it.

BOOM! BOOM! BOOM!

The ice was inches thick. Her tiny fists were no match for it. They couldn't even make a dent. Elsie opened her mouth and let out a scream. But underwater no one could hear her.

Just as she felt the life draining out of her, and that she was sinking down to a watery grave, she felt a surge underneath her. Something was pushing her up. It was Woolly! The girl was cradled between the mammoth's eyes as her sharp tusks smashed through the ice.

CRASH!

Elsie gasped. "AAH!"

"HOOOOO!?"

The girl was soaking wet and freezing cold but alive. Just. Elsie slid off the mammoth's face, landing on the ice with a thud.

"Oof!"

Although shivering and choking from the dirty Thames water, all Elsie could think about was her friend.

"WOOLLY!" she spluttered.

"HOOO!"

The mammoth's trunk was just poking out of the hole in the ice, as she desperately tried to breathe. With all her might, Elsie held on to it, so the animal wouldn't sink to her death.

"HOLD ON, WOOLLY! PLEASE!" she cried.

The girl knew it would be impossible for her to hoist this two-ton creature out of the river, but that didn't stop her from trying.

"HUH!"

And again.

"HUH!"

And again.

"HUH!"

"HOOO!"

All the strength in her body wasn't enough to save her friend's life. But they hadn't come this far for it to end now. There had to be a way to save her!

"SOMEBODY HELP!" screamed Elsie. Her voice echoed across the ice.

In the distance, she could see a handful of the Chelsea Pensioners in their distinctive scarlet coats and tricorne hats coming to the rescue!

Titch was leading from the front.

Under their arms the old soldiers were holding a thick rope, which snaked its way across the ice back to the ship.

Above their heads, the Zeppelin was circling for another attack.

"DIE, MONSTER, DIE!" yelled Buckshot.

RAT TAT TAT TAT TAT!

The machine gun blasted. Another hail of bullets sent shards of ice flying into the air.

KABOOM!

Slowly, the Zeppelin began coming round again to make another attack.

"THROW ME THE ROPE!" called out Elsie. The mammoth was sinking fast. Now only the tips of her tusks were bobbing out of the icy water. Elsie hooked the end of the rope round one of the tusks and tied it tight.

"HEAVE!" she ordered.

The old soldiers all gripped the rope and heaved

as hard as they could, just managing to pull the mammoth's head out of the water.

The animal spluttered, and let out a deafening **"HOO!"**

Aboard HMS *Victory* it was all hands on deck, as

the remaining pensioners took the end of the rope.

On the admiral's count…

"On three. One, two, three. Heave!"

…they all heaved, lifting the mammoth up and out of the freezing water. Woolly landed with a terrific thump on the ice.

DOOF!

"HOO!" she sighed.

"YES!" shouted Elsie. Looking behind Woolly, she saw two arcs of policemen and military policemen closing in on them. "LIFT THE SAILS!" she called out.

"Excuse me, young lady!" called back the admiral. "I am in charge of this ship!"

"All right, then! You say it!"

"LIFT THE SAILS!"

As the magnificent sails of HMS *Victory* were hoisted for the first time in years…

WHOOSH! WHOOSH! WHOOOSH!

…the gang on the ice pushed the mammoth back on to her feet.

"GO! GO! GO!" called out Elsie. She led the way across the ice to the ship, holding on to her friend so the mammoth would not slip.

In the sky, the Zeppelin was hovering round into position for yet another attack.

Behind the machine gun, Lady Buckshot had the mammoth in her sights once again.

RAT TAT TAT
TAT TAT!

"URGH!" screamed Titch as he clutched his stomach and sank to his knees.

Chapter 56

TITCH STITCH

"NOOOO!" screamed Dotty from the stern of HMS *Victory*. "TITCH!"

"Titch! No! Have you been hit?" asked Elsie.

"No. I've just got a stitch," he replied. Then in his most heroic tone he announced, "I'm not going to make it. You go on without me. Leave me here on the ice to die."

"*Die?* Titch! You've only got a stitch!"

"It's a bad one. A really bad one. But promise me one thing, young Elsie?"

"What, Titch?"

"Tell Dotty that... **I LOVE HER**. Urgh!" He clutched himself again.

Elsie shook her head. She might be the child here, but so often she felt more grown up than the grown-ups.

"You tell her, Titch!" said the girl, hooking her arm under his.

"What's happened to my darling?" called out Dotty from the ship.

"Titch has a stitch!" replied Elsie. Then the girl turned her attention back to the private. "Now stop being silly, Titch. Stitch or no stitch, we're all getting on that ship."

"I'll do my best, young miss."

The wind billowed the sails, and the ship's hull began creaking in the ice.

CRUNCH!

A huge ramp was lowered from HMS *Victory*, landing on the ice with a BOSH!

"WOOLLY FIRST!" shouted Elsie as she gathered the handful of pensioners to get behind the animal and push her up the ramp by her bottom.

As the boat rocked in the breaking ice, the ramp wobbled from side to side.

"HOOO!" hooted the mammoth.

"Nearly there, my friend!" called out Elsie, as she used all her might to make the final push over into the ship.

THUMP!

The wooden deck buckled a little under the mammoth's weight.

"HOOO!"

"HURRAH!" cried all on board, overjoyed that their large, hairy friend had made it.

Above HMS *Victory*, the Zeppelin was flying low.

"NOW I'VE GOT YOU, **ICE MONSTER**!" came a cry from the gondola.

RAT! TAT! TAT! TAT! TAT! TAT!

All the old soldiers hit the deck as HMS *Victory* was riddled with bullets.

POW! POW! POW!

"I'VE BEEN HIT!" yelled the admiral.

Dotty rushed over to him.

"Where?"

"MY LEG!"

"Which one?"

"The wooden one."

Indeed, there was a bullet lodged in there.

"Is it bleeding?" asked Dotty.

"Yes. Very badly."

"I can't see any blood!"

"No, it's just sawdust."

"Are you feeling any pain?"

"None at all. But I'm not going to let that blasted woman get away with this!"

· —✳︎— ·

Chapter 57

REVENGE

With its sails in full bloom, HMS *Victory* began forcing its way through the ice.

A cold and wet Elsie looked over the stern of the ship to see who was still following. In the distance, she could see something shaped like a sail speeding along the ice, overtaking the policemen. As it came closer, she realised the sail was multicoloured. It was, in fact, the balloon they had made of handkerchiefs (and one pair of bloomers).

"What...?" she muttered to herself.

It was only when the balloon got closer that she spotted the professor underneath it! He had attached the sail to his wheelchair, and was using the power of the wind to drag himself along.

"YOU CAN'T PUT A GREAT MAN DOWN!"

he called out. With one hand, he was steering the sail. In the other, he was holding the dart gun.

"I HAVE COME TO TAKE MY MONSTER BACK!

THIS IS REVENGE!"

"Oh no!" said Dotty. "This never ends!" she called out to the admiral. "Faster! Faster!"

"It's the ice!" the man called back. "It's so thick we can't go any faster!"

"LOOK!" She pointed to the professor.

"Maybe we can kill two birds with one stone," replied the admiral, setting a course straight for the newly built Tower Bridge.

Looking across to the riverbanks, Elsie noticed that London had woken up, and crowds were beginning to line the banks of the Thames. Much to her surprise, Londoners began clapping and cheering. They were clearly delighted to see this magnificent beast, the mammoth, brought back to life. And aboard Nelson's old warship no less.

"HURRAH!"

But there was a big problem. HMS *Victory*'s masts were too tall to fit under the bridge.

"We're not going to make it, Admiral!"

called out Titch from the bow of the ship.

"We need to get that bridge open!" the admiral called back.

Elsie spotted a group of a dozen children loitering on the bridge. The unmistakable figures of the **Sticky Fingers Gang**.

"ELSIE!" they shouted on seeing her.

"OPEN THE BRIDGE!" she shouted back. "UP! UP!"

Immediately, the gang began scaling the bridge to find the control room.

The Zeppelin was now just behind the ship, and gaining on them. Fast.

CLUNK! W H I R R !

Also gaining was the professor, who fired a poisoned dart.

PING!

It lodged into Buckshot's pith helmet.

"LOOK WHERE YOU'RE SHOOTING, YOU RUDDY FOOL, OR I'LL BLAST YOU TO SMITHEREENS!" she cried.

"THEN GET THAT PREPOSTEROUS CONTRAPTION OUT OF MY WAY!"

The professor fired again. This time the dart struck the Zeppelin's huge envelope of gas.

PPPFFFFFT!

There was a loud farting noise as air began escaping.

In a fury, Buckshot trained her machine gun on the professor.

RAT! TAT! TAT! TAT! TAT! TAT!!

"MISSED!" called out the professor.

"CHECK YOUR WHEELCHAIR, YOU OLD FOOL!"

He looked down. Indeed, she had blasted it out of existence. The professor was now skidding across the ice on his bottom.

In all the commotion, what neither had noticed was that Tower Bridge was beginning to rise.

The front mast of HMS *Victory* just clipped one of the sides of the bridge as it opened.

SCRAPE!

"HURRAH!" shouted the soldiers on the ship as HMS *Victory* passed under the magnificent bridge.

"HOOO!" hooted Woolly, joining in.

The admiral looked round to see not only Lady Buckshot looming right behind him in the Zeppelin, but also the professor skimming along the ice at the stern.

"Order those scallywags to lower the bridge. Quick smart!" ordered the admiral.

"DOWN! DOWN!" shouted the girl to her friends.

Right on cue, the bridge began to lower.

The machine gun blasted, once again ripping through the hull of the *Victory*.

RAT! TAT! TAT! TAT! TAT! TAT!

At the bottom of the Zeppelin, Lady Buckshot hollered her instructions to the pilot. "UP! UP!"

"Darn!" said the admiral. "She's not going to fall for it!"

A tethering cable was dangling down from the airship. Using her trunk, Woolly grabbed hold of the end.

"HOOO!"

"WOOLLY?" exclaimed Elsie in delight. This was one smart mammoth.

As the engines of the Zeppelin roared, the mammoth used all her strength to pull the flying machine down.

"HELP HER!" called out Elsie, and the old soldiers rushed to hold on to Woolly to stop her being pulled into the air.

"NOOO!" screamed Lady Buckshot, as the Zeppelin crashed straight into the bridge.

SMASH!

The envelope full of gas exploded in the air.

KABOOM!

"ARGH!" she cried as her gondola plunged right on to the professor, sending them both down into the icy waters of the Thames.

GURGLE! GURGLE! GURGLE!

PLOP! PLOP! PLOP!

GLUG! GLUG! GLUG!

"HURRAH!" shouted everyone on board the *Victory*.

"**HOOO!**" hooted Woolly.

The **Sticky Fingers Gang** all waved goodbye to Elsie.

"GOOD LUCK!" they shouted.

"THANK YOU!" she called back. "WE'LL NEED IT!"

The admiral addressed his crew. "Now, men, set sail for the North Pole!"

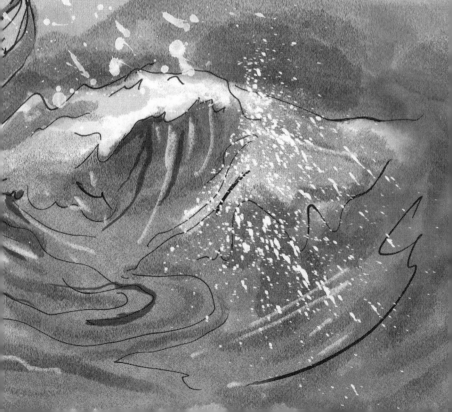

PART II

THE HIGH SEAS

Chapter 58

SLICING THROUGH THE ICE

"Which way is the North Pole, sir?" piped up Titch.

"Straight ahead, men!" commanded the admiral, pointing downriver. "Then when we reach the sea make a left!"

Just as the mammoth's arrival into the city had been a cause of great excitement, its departure was proving even more so. Word had spread fast, and soon it seemed like every Londoner was running along the

banks of the Thames, eager to be part of this awfully big adventure. The proud old admiral saluted them, which made the crowds cheer loudly.

"HURRAH!"

"HOOOO!" called out Woolly as she appeared to wave with her trunk.

This made the crowds go wild.

"HURRAH!"

It was a happy scene, and put joy into the hearts of all on board the *Victory*.

Titch sidled up to Dotty.

"I was very nearly a goner," he said.

"What happened, my love? I thought you'd been shot!" she replied.

"It was much, much worse than that. A stitch."

"A stitch?"

"Yes. A really bad stitch can be deadly."

"I didn't know that," replied the lady. "Maybe I need to kiss it better. Where does it hurt?"

The old soldier pointed to his lips. "Here."

They kissed. It was the shortest, sweetest kiss in the history of kisses. But the long-awaited meeting of their lips felt like fireworks to them, and they both looked light-headed as soon as they parted.

"I think I need a sit-down," said Dotty.

"I think I need a lie-down," said Titch.

"This is no time for kissing, sailors!" commanded the admiral. "We have a ship to sail!"

As he gave his orders, the men went to work. Soon HMS *Victory* picked up speed, and began slicing through the ice with ease. As the ship sailed through east London, getting nearer to the sea, the ice became thinner. HMS *Victory* began sailing faster and faster, until it passed out of the Thames Estuary and into the open sea.

"HURRAH!" cried the pensioners.

"HOOO!" cried Woolly.

"Port side!" ordered the admiral. This was the nautical term for the left side.

Waves were now hitting the ship, causing it to sway

from side to side. The mammoth had installed herself at the prow like an unofficial figurehead. Her trunk dangled down and covered the actual figurehead, which was a royal shield and a crown with a cherub on each side.

Elsie sidled up next to her friend. "Looking north again?" she said. The girl gazed out across the endless sea. The North Pole was thousands of miles away. "We'll get you home, Woolly. I promise."

With that, she stroked one of the mammoth's big furry ears. Woolly gently pushed her body against the girl as a way of saying thank you.

"HOO!" she cooed.

— ◆ —

Chapter 59

A DIAMOND
DUST OF STARS

Days passed at sea. HMS *Victory* sailed round the furthest tip of Scotland, and found herself alone in the deepest, darkest North Sea.

Weeks passed. As the ship travelled north, the sea grew rougher and rougher. Waves as tall as trees crashed over the *Victory*.

SPLISH!
SPLASH!
SPLOSH!

Everyone had to work together to stop the ship from sinking. Even Woolly. The mammoth hosed up the pools of water on the deck with her trunk, and sprayed them back overboard.

Another night descended on the *Victory* as at last they passed into calmer waters. The pensioners worked in shifts, and slept in the bunks below deck. Woolly was too large to fit, so when it was time to sleep Elsie stayed with her. Just like at the hospital, the pair of best friends snuggled up together.

"Goodnight, Woolly," Elsie would say.

"HOO!" Woolly would reply, which if translated from mammoth language means "Goodnight, Elsie". The girl would tuck herself in under the soft fur of Woolly's belly. The mammoth would then shuffle her legs together to protect her friend from the cold. Woolly made the softest, comfiest bed, and at night, as they lay together, Elsie felt that she was home. Looking up, she could see the diamond dust of stars in the sky.

Everything seemed so perfect.

It couldn't last.

And it didn't.

·⤙✳⤚·

Chapter 60

◆

SHIPS AHOY!

"SHIPS AHOY!" came the cry one morning from
the crow's nest of the *Victory*.

All the old soldiers scrambled to the stern of the
ship. There they jostled, eager to glimpse what their
comrade at the top of the mast had seen. The sound
of footsteps had woken up Elsie and Woolly too, and
they joined the line of pensioners. The admiral took
out his telescope.

A fleet of metal steamships stretched out across the
horizon.

"How many, Admiral?" asked Titch.

"A dozen, I would say."

"Can we outrun them?" asked Elsie.

"We can darn well try!"

"HURRAH!" shouted the men.

"HOO!" joined in Woolly.

The admiral called out his orders, to make this old ship go as fast as she possibly could.

HMS *Victory* felt as if it were taking flight as it soared across the sea.

Yet even at full speed it was no match for the modern steamships.

"They're gaining on us!" yelled Elsie.

"We're going at full speed!" replied the admiral. "Prepare the cannons!"

"With respect, Admiral, sir," piped up Titch, "we can't fire on our fellow countrymen!"

"No, you've got a point there," mused the admiral. "We'll be hanged as traitors."

"There must be something we can do!" exclaimed Elsie. "How many barrels of gunpowder have we got?"

Dotty counted them. "One, two, four, three, four, nine, three, seven, um, erm, six. A lot!" Counting was not her strong suit.

"A lot. Thank you, Dotty. I can count a dozen. A dozen barrels. What if we rolled them out to sea?"

"That's the most ridiculous idea I have ever heard, child! What a waste of jolly good gunpowder!" replied the admiral.

"I haven't finished yet!"

"OOH!" cooed the pensioners.

"I will have no 'oohing' on my ship!" thundered the admiral. "Do you understand me? Once you let sailors all 'ooh' at one another, heaven knows where it will lead!"

The old men nodded, still smirking at their own naughtiness.

"HOO!" called out Woolly.

"And less of your cheek, please," said the admiral to the mammoth.

"What I was going to say," continued Elsie, "is that we should roll out the barrels one by one. Then we wait until the ships close in. Then whoever is the best shot takes one of those muskets and shoots them."

"Shooting your own gunpowder?" thundered the admiral. "I have never heard such poppycock!"

"With respect, sir," began Titch timidly, "I think the girl is on to something. It will create a smokescreen!"

"A smokescreen?" spluttered the admiral.

"Yes! Then we will have a chance of losing the ships."

"Right, men, and erm, ladies, change tack," boomed the old sailor.

"When I give the order 'now', I want you to roll a barrel into the sea. Titch?"

"Yes, Admiral?"

"Do you know your way around a musket?"

"Well, I, er, um, the thing is…" He hesitated. The man was nervous. Only having the one medal (which was for service, the one all soldiers received), he had never thought of himself as a hero.

The last thing Titch wanted was to let everyone down.

Chapter 61

OPEN FIRE!

"Good!" replied the admiral. As usual, he hadn't been listening. "Titch, when I give the order 'fire' I want you to open fire on a barrel."

Poor Titch was shaking with nerves. It was clear he didn't want to be put under all this pressure.

One by one, the barrels were rolled into the sea.

ROLL

PLOP!

ROLL

PLOP!

ROLL

PLOP!

Soon there were a dozen barrels of gunpowder bobbing around in the water as the British naval fleet approached.

"Titch? Are you ready?" asked the admiral.

The poor private was struggling, trying to ram the gunpowder down the antique musket. "One moment, sir!"

Dotty tried to help by passing him the shot.

"I can do it!" he snapped.

"TITCH!" called out the admiral.

"Ready, sir!"

Titch raised the musket.

"FIRE!"

The private took a deep breath. This was his moment to prove them all wrong. To prove that he could be a hero after all. Trembling, he did something he'd never done before in all his years as a soldier. He pulled the trigger.

CLICK!

Nothing happened.

"Sorry, sir, I'm half-cocked!"

"FIRE!"

BANG!

The force of the blast threw Titch off his aim.

Instead of the shot firing across the sea towards the barrel, it skimmed over Woolly's head, parting her fur…

"HOOO!"

…before blasting a huge hole in one of HMS *Victory*'s sails.

"You ruddy fool!" raged the admiral. "I'll have you court-martialled for this!"

"I'm useless!" said Titch, bowing his head in defeat.

"Give that musket to me, Private," ordered the admiral.

"Let him have another go!" pleaded Dotty.

"Are we at the funfair?" asked the brigadier.

"I had me chance and I blew it!" Titch wailed in despair.

"No, Titch!" piped up Elsie. "You can do it. I know you can."

She turned to the admiral. "Please?"

The admiral had a soft spot for the girl.

"All right, then," he huffed. "But there are a dozen barrels and only a dozen cartridges. If he fails, that's it."

"No pressure, my love," added Dotty, somewhat unhelpfully.

The admiral let out a long sigh. "Fire at will, Private."

Titch loaded the musket, and aimed. He took a deep breath, closed his eyes and fired.

BANG!

This shot skimmed across the sea.

KABOOM!

The barrel of gunpowder exploded.

A thick cloud of black smoke appeared.

"HURRAH!" shouted the old soldiers on the deck of HMS *Victory*.

"HOOO!" hooted the mammoth.

"YOU DID IT, TITCH!" yelled Elsie.

"My hero!" added Dotty.

"One down. Eleven to go!" said Titch.

"FIRE!" ordered the admiral.

KABOOM!

And another.

KABOOM!

Another.

KABOOM!

KABOOM!

KABOOM!

Three in a row.

Bull's-eye!

KABOOM!

KABOOM!

YES!

KABOOM!

On a roll now.

KABOOM!

Easy.

KABOOM!

Final one…

KABOOM!

Against all the odds, Titch had hit every single barrel. Now there was a huge curtain of black smoke stretching out across the sea.

"HURRAH!" shouted the soldiers.

"HOOO!" added Woolly.

·~✻~·

Chapter 62

◆

DOWN BUT
NOT OUT

"**S**ILENCE!" ordered the admiral. "Let's listen for their ships!"

Everyone on board fell silent. Far off, they could hear the sound of horns hooting and engines grinding.

KERRANG!

There was even the sound of metal hitting metal as ships collided.

BASH!
BANG!
WALLOP!

"Oops!" said the admiral.

"We got 'em!" exclaimed Dotty.

"**HOO!**" shouted Woolly, punching her trunk into the air in triumph.

"They're the British naval fleet," began the admiral.

"The best in the world. They're down but they're not out. The smoke will lift soon. We must act fast. We need to change course if we're going to lose them. STARBOARD HO!"

All on board went to work to make the ship dramatically change course to the right. Even the mammoth was getting the hang of sailing now. Using her trunk, she grabbed hold of the wheel, spinning it hard to the right. The ship leaned the other way so fast that the old soldiers tumbled over. Woolly fell on top of the admiral.

"HOOO!"

DUMF!

"OOF!" cried the admiral. "GET THIS GIANT FUR BALL OFF ME!"

Elsie smirked as she and all available hands on deck prised the mammoth off their leader.

"Thank goodness I'm not planning on having any more children!" muttered the admiral as he clambered to his foot. He limped over to the stern of the ship.

DUFF! DUFF! DUFF!

Next, he took out his telescope and studied the sea behind them. The curtain of smoke was slowly lifting. Elsie sidled up to him and Woolly followed. The mammoth was intrigued. She plucked the telescope out of his hands with her trunk.

SWIPE!

"GET OFF THAT!"

he snapped before snatching it back. He then turned to Elsie. "Please try and control your pet mammoth."

"I'll try, sir," she replied with a grin.

"I can't see any ships," he said. "I think we've done it. My goodness, we've done it."

Just then, Elsie spotted a shape poking out of the curtain of smoke.

"THERE!" she shouted.

The admiral put the telescope back up to his eye. "BLAST! One of them has got through."

"We can't give up, Admiral," said the girl.

"NEVER! Now listen up, men! And, erm, woman, and, of course, girl…" began the admiral.

"HOOO!" added Woolly, not wanting to be left out.

"Yes, yes, apologies," replied the admiral, rolling his eyes. "And listen up, mammoth! One of the ships has got through."

"OH NO!" came a chorus of replies.

"We have to prepare for the worst. In less than an hour, they will have reached us. We must be ready to be boarded. Men, and, erm, woman, and, of course, girl…"

"HOO!" Woolly reminded him.

"…and, who can forget, mammoth. We have no more shot. The gunpowder is gone. But you must arm yourselves with whatever you can lay your hands on!"

"YES, SIR!" came a chorus of replies.

"Good luck, men, and everyone else not contained in that umbrella term!"

Immediately, the deck of HMS *Victory* was a hive of activity, as all on board went about arming themselves. There weren't enough cutlasses to go around, so most of the soldiers picked up brooms and mops.

Slowly but surely, the British naval ship that was still pursuing them came into focus. She was the mighty HMS *Argonaut.**

With four huge funnels pumping smoke from its coal engine, the *Argonaut* was powering through the waves right towards the *Victory*.

With their makeshift weapons in their hands, the old soldiers were ready for the worst. The admiral approached Elsie. "You are but a child. I think it best you go below deck."

---

* *Named after the crew of Jason's ship, the* Argo, *in ancient Greek mythology.*

"Are you kidding?" replied the girl, reaching for a long wooden sail batten. "I wouldn't miss this for the world."

"We'll make a sailor of you yet!" said the admiral. He took off his wooden leg and brandished it, ready to do battle. Forgetting he couldn't stand up on his one leg, he wobbled for a moment before hitting the deck.

THUMP!

Chapter 63

SURRENDER!

"**S**URRENDER!" boomed a voice over the loud-hailer from HMS *Argonaut* as it drew up alongside the *Victory*.

"**NEVER!**" came a chorus of voices from HMS *Victory*.

"SORRY. I DIDN'T QUITE CATCH THAT!"

"**WE SAID 'NEVER'.**"

"DID YOU SAY 'NEVER'?"

"**YES!**"

"SORRY, IT'S HARD TO HEAR. YOU DON'T HAVE A LOUD-HAILER YOU COULD USE, DO YOU?"

"**NO!**"

"WHAT WAS THAT?"

"WE SAID 'NO'!"

"THAT'S A SHAME."

"WE KNOW."

"SORRY, WHAT WAS THAT?"

"WE SAID, 'WE KNOW'."

"THANK YOU. NOW OUR ORDERS ARE TO RETURN THE **ICE MONSTER** TO LONDON. IT IS THE PROPERTY OF HER MAJESTY THE QUEEN."

All the old soldiers looked to Elsie. She told them, "Woolly isn't the property of anyone."

"OH NO, IT'S NOT!" began the chorus from HMS *Victory*.

"OH YES, IT IS!" came the voices back.

"OH NO, IT'S NOT."

"OH YES, IT IS."

"Are we at the pantomime?" asked the brigadier.

"IF YOU RETURN THE CREATURE TO US, THEN THERE IS NO NEED FOR US TO OPEN FIRE. DO YOU SURRENDER?"

"NO!"

"I AM PRETTY SURE THAT WAS A 'NO'."

"YES!"

"SORRY, YES THAT WAS A 'NO', OR YES BECAUSE IT WAS A 'YES'?"

"IT WAS A 'NO'!"

"THANK YOU!"

"OUR PLEASURE!"

"THANK YOU."

"NOT AT ALL."

"THEN PREPARE FOR BATTLE!"

"Cor, that took 'em long enough," muttered Dotty.

HMS *Argonaut* inched closer to HMS *Victory*. The young sailors looked across at the old soldiers.

The two groups nodded to each other politely. They were all British after all. Finally, the captain of HMS *Argonaut* gave the order. "ATTACK!"

Chapter 64

A POOL OF BLOOD

The young sailors leaped from one ship to another with ease. They landed on the deck of the *Victory*, brandishing their rifles.

"CHARGE!" shouted the admiral, as he led his pensioners into battle. The old soldiers were brave, and attacked the young sailors with their cutlasses, mops and brooms.

CLUNK!

CLINK!

CLANK!

They went straight for the rifles, trying to force them to the floor.

Meanwhile, Dotty had found an old tin bucket, and was bashing the young sailors over the head with it.

BISH!

BASH!

BOSH!

Many were knocked out by the force of her blows.

"OUCH!"

THUD!

"OOF!"

THUD!

"ARGH!"

THUD!

Meanwhile, Elsie attacked the invaders by whacking them on their bottoms with her sail batten.

THWACK!

"AH!"

THWUCK!

"AAHH!!"

THWOCK!

"AAAAAHHHH!"

A smile spread across her face. This was fun.

Woolly joined in too.

"HOO!"

With her tusks, the mammoth scooped up a sailor, before dropping him in the sea.

"NOOO!"

PLOP!

As Elsie battled on, out of the corner of her eye she could see a cannon on HMS *Argonaut* swivelling round. Now it was pointing straight at the mammoth. The captain gave the order.

"FIRE AT WILL!"

"NOOOOO!" screamed Elsie as she put her hands up in the air to shield her friend. The gunner fired, and a huge net shot across the decks of the *Victory*, trapping the mammoth in its web.

"HOO!" roared Woolly. The poor thing was distressed, and began bucking and thrashing around.

HOO!

The more she did so, the more tangled she became.

"HOO! HOO!"

"WOOLLY! WOOLLY!" cried the girl,
trying to calm the creature down, to no avail.

The mammoth lurched across the deck, bashing
into people and things.

"HOO!"

She swung round and knocked a sailor to the floor.

DOOF!

"ARGH!"

Another was trodden on by a giant prehistoric foot.

BOOF!

"OUCH!"

A third sailor became tangled in the net, and was dragged across the deck.

"HELP!"

Still clutching his rifle, the sailor's finger snagged on the trigger. A shot rang out.

BANG!

All was quiet and still on board the *Victory*.

Woolly was quiet and still too. She stopped thrashing around and stood motionless for a moment, before she keeled over and landed with a deafening THUD.

A pool of blood spread across the deck.

"WOOLLY! NOOOOOO!" screamed Elsie.

Chapter 65

HARD RAIN

The old soldiers and the young sailors all worked together to untangle the mammoth from the net. As soon as the captain of HMS *Argonaut* had hauled two of his sailors out of the North Sea, he stepped on board the HMS *Victory* to help.

"I'm so sorry this has happened," said the captain.

Elsie put her hands over the wound in Woolly's chest to stop the flow of blood.

"WHY DID YOU SHOOT HER?" she cried. "WHY?"

There was no answer.

"Somebody do something!" she begged.

Dotty put her ear to the animal's mouth. "I can't hear her breathing. I'm so sorry, Elsie. I know you loved her. And she loved you. But this is the end of the story."

"NOOO!" yelled Elsie.

BO**O**M!

Thunder rolled across the sea. Ahead, black clouds were swirling. A storm was coming.

"Sail into the storm!" ordered Elsie.

The admiral looked aghast. "No. It would be the end of us all."

"It's the only way we can save her."

"By sailing into a storm?" demanded the admiral.

"We used lightning to restart her heart before. Maybe we can do it again."

Dotty rushed over to where Elsie was trying to stop the flow of blood.

"Let me take over!" she said.

The lady pushed the end of her mop right into the wound, and the flow of blood slowed.

"We can tow you into the storm!" offered the captain of the *Argonaut*.

"No," replied the admiral. "It's too dangerous. You young sailors have got your whole lives ahead of you."

He turned to the pensioners.

"Men. Are you all with me?"

"YES, SIR!" came the reply.

"Good luck!" said the captain, and he and the admiral saluted each other. "We will make sure *Queen Victoria* is told all about your bravery."

The captain led his men back on board the *Argonaut* as the admiral called out his orders.

"Set course for the storm!"

The men went to work, and soon HMS *Victory* was flying into the darkness ahead.

"Elsie?" began Dotty. "Do you know what you're doing? We don't have a balloon or metal wire or anything."

"I know." The girl choked, fighting back a river of tears. "But there must be a way."

Her eyes searched the deck of the *Victory*. At the bow, she spotted something.

"See that metal chain, Titch?"

"Yes!" replied the old soldier. "That's for dropping the anchor."

"Put the anchor right next to Woolly's heart, and then pass me the end of the chain."

"Right-ho!"

Titch scuttled over to the bow, and with the help of his fellow pensioners he dragged the anchor and chain over to where the mammoth was lying.

Elsie took the end of the chain and wrapped it round her wrist. Then she placed a cutlass between her teeth like a pirate, and with her monkey feet began climbing the rigging.

"Where do you think you're going?" asked Dotty.

"The crow's nest, of course," Elsie replied, her speech hard to understand thanks to the cutlass in her mouth.

As the ship crashed up and down on the angry waves…

THRUMP! THRUMP! THRUMP!

…Elsie climbed up and up and up. Once at the top, she clambered into the crow's nest and looked straight ahead into the storm.

"Come on!" she whispered to the sky. *"Give me everything you've got."*

All the way up there at the tallest point of the *Victory*, the rolling of the ship in the waves became exaggerated. Elsie found herself holding on for dear life.

She looked down to see the admiral at the wheel, holding on tightly so the waves didn't hurl him into the sea. Hard rain was flying into the girl's eyes. It was a struggle to keep them open. Soon she was soaked to the skin. The wind wound around her, and the clouds skimmed her hair.

"Straight ahead, Admiral!" she ordered.

"Aye, aye, Captain Elsie!" he called back up.

BOOM!

Thunder rumbled across the black sky.

"Come on, lightning!" the girl whispered. "I know you're in there somewhere."

As if on cue, a flash of lightning illuminated the sky.

KRAZZLE!

"Are you sure you know what you're doing?" called up Dotty.

"No. This is madness!"

"Good madness or bad madness?"

"Good, I hope!"

Elsie lifted the cutlass high into the air.

"But the lightning, Elsie. It could kill you!" shouted Dotty.

"If it does, promise you'll look after Woolly for me. Make sure she gets to the North Pole? PLEASE?"

"Don't do this!"

"Why?"

"I love you, Elsie. You're like a grandma to me."

"I think you mean granddaughter, Dotty, and I love you too, but I have to save my friend. Promise you'll look after her."

"I promise!"

A bolt of lightning hit the front sail, and it burst into flames.

BOOM!

"FIRE ON BOARD!" shouted the admiral as his men struggled to put it out.

"Nearly!" whispered Elsie. She stretched her arm as high as it would go, and closed her eyes.

"COME ON!" she shouted.

A bolt of lightning struck the tip of the cutlass.

"AAH!" cried Elsie as the electricity sizzled through her.

Chapter 66

A WATERY GRAVE

The bolt of lightning passed through the girl and shot down the metal chain. The anchor had been pushed against the lifeless creature's chest, and now it delivered a thump of electricity to Woolly's heart.

DUMF!

Elsie slumped to her knees at the highest point of the ship, and the mammoth's legs twitched.

One eye opened.

Then another.

"SHE'S ALIVE!" shouted Dotty. "Do you hear me, Elsie? Elsie?"

As thunder and lightning boomed around them, Dotty and Titch looked up to the crow's nest.

"NOOOO!" screamed Dotty when she saw the girl slumped over the side, lifeless.

"You look after Woolly!" cried
Titch as he began climbing up the
rigging.

The boat was now swinging
wildly from side to side, and the
higher he scrabbled, the more he
felt he was going to be tossed into a
watery grave.

Eventually, he reached the crow's
nest. Elsie was now lying motionless
on the floor.

"ELSIE? ELSIE?" he cried, but
there was no response. Titch scooped her
up in his arms, and put her over his shoulder.
Then he made the hazardous climb down
the rigging, and laid her out on the deck of the
ship.

Elsie's face was blackened and, despite the rain, her
hair and clothes were smoking.

It seemed that the electric bolt, which had given the
mammoth life, had taken life away from the girl.

411

On seeing her friend laid out like this, Woolly scrambled over to her.

First, the mammoth tried to rock her friend awake with her foot.

"HOO!"

Elsie just flopped from side to side.

Next, she licked the girl's face with her tongue.

"HOO!"

A white streak appeared on her skin.

Dotty burst into floods of tears and held Elsie's lifeless body close to hers. "No! No! Please!"

Titch put his arms round her. "I think she's left us."

Chapter 67

HEADS BOWED

The pensioners stood around the body with their heads bowed and their hats held close to their chests.

All was quiet and still on the deck of the *Victory*.

However, the mammoth was not giving up on her friend.

"HOO!"

To everyone's surprise, Woolly placed her trunk over the girl's nose and mouth, and blew air into her.

"What's the beast doing?" said the admiral, as he tried to keep steering the *Victory* through the storm.

"I think she's trying to recessuss… resasstate… restitiute… blow air into Elsie!" replied Dotty.

"Her chest is moving up and down!" exclaimed Titch.

"Thank the good Lord for his mercy!" cried out Dotty. "She's alive!"

Elsie's eyes opened. A huge wet furry trunk was staring back at her. At first, she didn't know where she was, or even who she was.

"What the…?"

But, as soon as she realised who was looming over her, she took the trunk in her hands and kissed it.

"Oh, thank you, thank you, thank you, Woolly! I love you!"

The mammoth wrapped her trunk round the girl, and pulled her close for a cuddle.

"HURRAH!" cried the old soldiers.

"This is all very well and good, gentlemen, and, er, lady, and, girl, and, of course, mammoth, and so on and so forth," began the admiral, "but can I politely remind you that we are still sailing through the heart of a storm? It's going to take every last man, every last person and prehistoric animal for us to survive this! Back to work at once!"

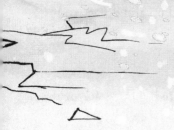

PART III

THE
NORTH
POLE

Chapter 68

◆

BATTERED AND BRUISED

Battered and bruised, HMS *Victory* eventually sailed into calmer waters.

An **icy wind** blew across the ship. They were moving closer and closer to the North Pole. A shout came down from the crow's nest.

"ICEBERG AHOY!"

Elsie whispered into the mammoth's ear. "We're getting close, Woolly."

The mammoth nodded her head up and down, and called out, **"HOO!"**

"Very close."

The admiral expertly navigated HMS *Victory* through the maze of ice.

"LAND AHOY!" came another shout from above.

"HOOO!" hooted Woolly. Somehow, she knew she was going home.

The ship stopped alongside the edge of the ice, causing a huddle of walruses to scatter into the water.

PLOP! PLOP! PLOP!

After weeks at sea, the mammoth was eager to step out on to solid ice. Her entire body was swaying with excitement.

"Not long now, Woolly!" said Elsie.

As soon as it was safe, she led her friend down the gangplank and on to the ice. Immediately, the mammoth rolled on to her back, rubbing herself on the snow. Elsie thought it looked like fun, so joined in too. She even fashioned a snowball, which she lobbed at Woolly.

BIFF!

In return, the mammoth hoovered up some snow with her trunk, and sprayed it at the girl.

419

PFFF!

Dotty and Titch looked on from the deck of the *Victory*, like proud grandparents.

When Elsie and Woolly both began to tire, the girl decided it was time to say goodbye. She gave her friend the biggest cuddle she could.

"I'm going to miss you so much," she whispered into the mammoth's ear.

Woolly shook her head.

Whatever did the animal mean?

She reached out her trunk, and took the girl by the hand, and began tugging her along.

"Woolly wants me to go with her," Elsie called out to those on the ship. "But where?"

Chapter 69

◆

SOME KIND OF MACHINE

"We're coming too!" exclaimed Dotty, dragging Titch by the hand.

"Do we have to? I am f-f-f-freezing!" he moaned.

"Come on!"

The lady dragged her beloved off the ship, and on to the ice.

"Wait there, please!" Dotty called back to the admiral.

"We were going to go straight back to London," replied the admiral sarcastically, "but, now you ask, we'll wait."

"Thank you kindly!" said the lady.

Woolly led her three friends across the ice. Soon they had lost sight of the *Victory*.

"We'll have to try and remember which way we came," remarked Titch.

"Yes. Turn left at the mound of snow," replied Dotty unhelpfully.

Underneath the ice, there was the sound of something whirring.

RURRR!

It stopped Woolly in her tracks.

"HOOO!" she cried softly, clearly spooked.

"What's that?" said Elsie.

"What's what?" asked Dotty.

"That sound," replied the girl. She put her ear down to the ice.

"Maybe it's a killer whale," suggested Titch.

Woolly shook her head.

"No," replied the girl. "This is some kind of machine."

All four stood still and silent.

Suddenly, there was the deafening noise of something grinding through the ice.

DRERRRRR!

Ahead of them a metal nose burst out.

SMASH!

"HOOOO!" screamed Woolly.

"What's *that*?" gasped Elsie.

"It's one of them submarines," replied Titch.

"What's it doing here?" asked Elsie.

"And who's going to sweep up all the ice?" remarked Dotty.

The underwater craft forced its way up to the surface, and bobbed on the sea for a moment.

"Shall we make a run for it?" suggested Elsie.

"No. Let's stand our ground," replied Titch.

"My hero," said Dotty.

A hatch opened on top of the submarine, and a pith helmet emerged, followed by a gnarled face, which seemed to have been burned in an explosion.

"Well, well, well. Fancy meeting you here," snarled the lady.

It was Lady Buckshot. She was chomping on a cigar and wielding a shotgun.

"HOO!" cried Woolly.

"Yes, how peculiar!" replied Dotty.

"Maybe we should have made a run for it," said Titch.

"Thought you could kill me off, did you?" called out the big-game hunter, as she stepped down from her submarine on to the ice. "Thought your little stunt with Tower Bridge was clever, did you?"

"Mmm," mused Dotty. "Probably not saying the right thing here, but yes, I did, actually."

"SILENCE!"

"You asked the question!"

"It was a rhetorical question!"

"What's that?"

"You don't know what a rhetorical question is?"

"No."

"SILENCE! That was also a rhetorical question!"

"We're going round in circles now."

"Right, I'll shoot you first!"

Elsie stepped in front of Dotty.

"Never," said the girl.

Titch stepped in front of Elsie.

"**NEVER!**" he said.

Then Woolly swept them both aside with her trunk.

"**HOOO!**" she hooted at the hunter.

"I'll just stay here at the back if that's all right with everyone," announced Dotty.

"Oh, for goodness' sake!" thundered Buckshot, spitting out her cigar and pointing her shotgun at each of them in turn. "I WILL KILL YOU ALL!"

· ⭑ ·

Chapter 70

✦

BEHIND YOU!

Buckshot cocked her shotgun.

CLICK!

"Don't you fools see how good all your heads would look on my wall?" she called out.

"I rather like my head attached to my body," Elsie called back. "And so does Woolly!"

"HOO!" The mammoth nodded in agreement.

"Woolly?" mocked Buckshot. "The monster has a name!"

"She's not a monster; she's a manmoth," said Dotty.

"A what?" asked Buckshot.

"A MANMOTH! ARE YOU DEAF?"

"It'll take too long to explain," said Elsie.

"Fine. I don't have the time anyway. Prepare to die…"

Titch put his hand up in the air. "Excuse me, lady?"

"What now?"

"There's a polar bear behind you," he lied.

"No, there isn't," said Dotty.

"Shut up!" he hissed.

"Yes, there is!" Elsie continued the lie. "A really big one."

"I'm not falling for that old chestnut!" thundered Buckshot.

"HOO!" hooted Woolly, pointing with her trunk at the spot where this imaginary bear might be.

"Oh, I get it," said Dotty. "There's a really big brown bear…"

"White bear!" hissed Titch.

"…white bear behind you!"

"It would look great on your wall," added Elsie. Behind her, she could sense the mammoth was straining.

"What are you doing, Woolly?" whispered Elsie.

The mammoth had shut her eyes tight in concentration.

Finally, it came.

A bottom burp.

GGGGGGRRRRRUUUUURRRRR!

A bottom burp that sounded exactly like the growl of a bear.

The noise made Buckshot turn round and look.

It gave the gang of four just enough time to rush at her. Titch rugby-tackled her, and she fell to the ice.

THUMP!

"ARGH!"

Dotty sat on her, so she was trapped.

"GET ORFF ME, YOU PEASANT!"

Next, Elsie snatched the shotgun from her, and threw it as far away as she could, so that it landed in deep snow.

"GIVE ME THAT BACK!"

Last, Woolly lolloped forward, and with her trunk grabbed the lady by her ankle.

"WHAT ARE YOU DOING, YOU BEAST?"

Guessing what was to come, Elsie helped Dotty off Buckshot.

Then Woolly dangled her would-be killer in the air.

"HELP!" she cried.

"Not on your nelly!" said Dotty.

The mammoth lifted the hunter high in the air and began swinging her in circles.

"AAARRRGGGHHH!!!"

yelled Buckshot.

The circles became faster and faster.

WHIRR!

Soon Buckshot became nothing more than a blur.

"AAAAARRRRGGGGGHHHHH!!!!!"

"Now let go!" said Elsie.

The mammoth did what she was told.

"NNNNNNNOOOOOOOOOO!"

cried Buckshot as she spun through the air like a boomerang. W H I Z Z !

Unlike a boomerang, she didn't come back.

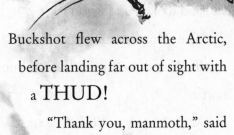

Buckshot flew across the Arctic, before landing far out of sight with a THUD!

"Thank you, manmoth," said Dotty. "That woman was beginning to get on my nerves."

Chapter 71

SMOTHERING
to DEATH

Woolly led the three humans for many more miles across the ice. North. North. North. As night fell, the entire sky lit up red and green and purple.

"Wow! This is beautiful!" said Elsie as she stopped still and looked up in wonder.

"The Northern Lights, they're called," replied Titch. "You can only see them if you travel really far north."

"Well, I went to Yorkshire to visit my aunt Maud and I never saw 'em," said Dotty.

Titch shook his head. "I mean *really* far north."

"As far as I'm concerned, Yorkshire *is* really far north. It took me hours on the train. Now, where's the manmoth taking us?"

"North!" replied Elsie. "North, north, north!"

"Are there going to be any shops?" asked Dotty.

"I don't think so," said Titch.

"I don't need nothing fancy, just a cup of tea, some sandwiches or cakes."

"No. Just more ice."

"Shame!" Dotty said. "I'm getting rather peckish."

They climbed to the top of a tall snowdrift and looked down into a valley.

"How much longer?" moaned Dotty.

"HOOO!" hooted Woolly. She pointed ahead with her trunk, before galloping down the drift.

"Something tells me we're nearly there!" replied the girl as she chased after her friend.

"HOOO!"

"Hoooo!" joined in Elsie.

"Nearly where?" asked Dotty.

"I don't know," replied Titch. He took her hand and led her down the drift.

Ahead, Elsie could see something was sticking out of the snow. On closer inspection, she realised it was a flag. A British flag. Next to it were a series of pegs, marking out a large rectangular shape in the ice. It looked almost like a grave.

"This must be where they found Woolly!" exclaimed Elsie.

"**HOOO!**" hooted the mammoth, miming digging with her foot.

"Why the blazes has the manmoth brought us all the way here?" grumbled Dotty.

"There must be a reason, Dotty. Trust me," replied the girl.

As if on cue, the coloured lights that were shooting across the sky descended to the ground. The wind

whipped up the snow, and soon it swirled all around them. The four were in the centre of a spiralling snowstorm. It soon became impossible for Elsie, Dotty and Titch to keep their eyes open, and they could hardly breathe. All they could do was huddle close to the mammoth in fear.

"This is the end, Dotty!" spluttered Titch as snow swirled into his mouth. "I need to tell you that I…"

"Tell me what?" asked the lady.

"If you would just let me finish!"

"Woolly wouldn't have brought us all out here to die!" shouted Elsie. "There must be a good reason."

The mammoth wrapped her trunk round the girl.

"HOO!" she cried.

"Hold me close," said Elsie. "Please."

This felt like the end.

The storm moved in. The blizzard was smothering them. They could no longer see, or feel, or hear.

Elsie just managed to prise her eyes open for a moment.

Huge shapes were appearing out of the snowstorm.

"LOOK!" cried Elsie.

They were not alone.

Chapter 72

A PERFECT CIRCLE

A dozen figures were emerging from the storm, as tall and wide as ships.

Dotty and Titch struggled to open their eyes. When they did, the most magical sight greeted them.

A herd of mammoths.

"I wouldn't want to have to clean up after all that lot," mused Dotty.

"Is this real?" asked Titch.

"I don't know," replied Elsie. "But it's beautiful!"

"HOO!" cried Woolly.

As if by magic, the snowstorm moved outwards from where the gang of four were huddled. They found themselves standing in a perfect circle of calm as a wall of swirling snow surrounded them.

Slowly, Woolly broke away from the humans, and approached the herd. One of the mammoths stepped

forward and reached out its trunk. Woolly did the same, and the two trunks curled round each other in the most loving way.

All the other mammoths lifted up their trunks and let out a chorus of **HOOs.**

HOO! HOO! HOO!

HOO! HOO!

HOO! **HOO!** HOO!

HOO!

HOO! HOO! HOO!

HOO! **HOO!**

HOO! HOO!

Teardrops ran down Elsie's face. They were happy tears. They were sad tears. Happy because she knew her friend was finally home. Sad because she knew this was goodbye.

Woolly turned round, and with her trunk beckoned Elsie over.

"HOO!"

The girl took a deep breath, and paced through the deep snow. Woolly wrapped her trunk round her friend, and pushed her close to the much bigger mammoth in front of them. Elsie was scared at first, but the giant mammoth wrapped her trunk lovingly round the girl. The three of them embraced. Immediately, the girl knew exactly who this was.

"Woolly. It's so great to finally meet your ma," said Elsie, choking back tears.

Both animals nodded their heads, and let out tender sighs.

"HOO!" sounded the largest animal behind them. It was time to go. The herd turned to leave.

The mother mammoth gently pushed her offspring towards the girl. There was just time for one last embrace. Elsie buried her head in her friend's fur, and wrapped her arms round her. In return, Woolly licked the girl's face with her rough tongue. It was a sweet, if slobbery, kiss.

Elsie whispered into the mammoth's ear, "I love you, Woolly. I'm never going to forget you. You won't ever forget me, will you?"

"HOO!" Woolly sighed.

"Hoo!" replied Elsie.

The girl reached out her hand and stroked Woolly's fur as the animal started to move away. This was the very last touch. Elsie watched as one by one the herd faded into the wall of snow. Woolly looked back one last time, and waved with her trunk, and then she too disappeared.

Tears rolled down Elsie's face again, as Dotty and Titch put their arms round the girl and held her tight. The storm passed as quickly as it had appeared, leaving the three alone on the Arctic wasteland.

PART IV

HOME

Chapter 73

✦

HEADLINES
ACROSS THE WORLD

If the long sail back to London was sombre, the journey up the Thames was anything but. All of London turned out to watch HMS *Victory*, which had seen off the entire British naval fleet, make its way along the river. The news of the mammoth's adventures had made headlines all across the world.

ORPHAN GIRL BRINGS MAMMOTH BACK TO LIFE!

MONSTER ON THE LOOSE!

GANG'S DARING ESCAPE FROM LONDON

The London Chronicle HMS VICTORY STOLEN!

The Evening Standard CHELSEA PENSIONERS BREAK OUT OF ROYAL HOSPITAL

Folk lined the banks to wave and cheer, and this lifted Elsie's mood a little. During the long voyage, the girl missed her friend terribly. She had grown accustomed to the mammoth's smell and sound and touch. She yearned for her trunk to be wrapped round her again. It was like a part of her was missing.

A month or more had gone by since they'd left London. The ice over the Thames had melted away, and HMS *Victory* made fast progress towards the centre of London.

Despite seeing the obvious delight of the crowds, all on board were nervous as the ship came into dock. A pack of policemen, led by Commissioner Barker, of course, were waiting on the riverbank for them.

"Don't you worry, officers. We only, ahem, borrowed the *Victory*. Took her for a quick spin," the admiral called over.

Barker's face soured. His lip quivered in barely disguised rage, causing his tiny moustache to twitch.

"Our orders are to take you straight to Buckingham Palace," he announced. "Her Majesty the Queen wants a word with you!"

The pensioners all gulped. By the sound of it, they were all in

deep,

deep

trouble.

•⤙✱⤚•

Chapter 74

A FLEET OF CARRIAGES

A fleet of horse-drawn carriages raced across London to Buckingham Palace. Elsie sat between Dotty and Titch in the first one. Both grown-ups looked sick with nerves.

Dotty pulled out a handkerchief and spat on it. "Elsie, I just need to give you a quick wash." She then proceeded to furiously polish the girl's face.

"GET OFF ME!" yelled Elsie.

"You're meeting the Queen! When was the last time you had a bath?"

"A what?"

"That's what I thought!"

The fleet of carriages passed through the tall iron gates into the grounds of Buckingham Palace. Elsie, Dotty and Titch all pressed their faces up against the window to get a better look.

"WOW!" exclaimed the girl.

"It's magnificent," added Titch.

"It could be fit for royalty," remarked Dotty.

"It is fit for royalty!" said Titch. "The royals live here."

"They must have come from a very rich family," observed the lady.

The carriage stopped outside the entrance to the palace itself. A footman opened the carriage door, and the three stepped out on to the red carpet. All the old soldiers put on their tricorne hats and white gloves,

and straightened their scarlet coats. They formed a neat line, and marched into Buckingham Palace.

Elsie's eyes were dazzled by the riches. Never in her wildest dreams could she have believed anyone lived like this. Gold and marble and velvet spread across every space. Oil paintings, sculptures and ornaments lined the hallways. She wanted to stop and marvel at every last one, but there wasn't time. Her Majesty the Queen was waiting.

"Needs a good dust," remarked Dotty. "I've counted three cobwebs."

"Shush!" shushed Titch.

Eventually, a tall pair of wooden doors was opened by the Queen's attendant Abdul.

"Her Majesty has been expecting you," he announced.

At the far end of the room was a little old lady, sitting alone on a chair with a blanket over her knees. Her skin was as white as snow, her dress was black, and her white hair crouched on top of her head in a tidy bun.

It was Queen Victoria. Unsmiling, she looked Elsie straight in the eye.

"So, you must be the urchin who stole my mammoth?"

Chapter 75

◆

AN AUDIENCE
WITH THE QUEEN

For the first time in her life Elsie was too shy to speak, so she just nodded.

"It weren't just her that stole the manmoth!" said Dotty. "I done it an' all."

"Don't forget your manners," hissed the admiral. "It's 'I done it and all, ma'am'. 'Ma'am' not 'Marm'. It rhymes with 'ham' or 'jam'."

"I done it an' all, ham," said Dotty.

Titch shook his head in despair.

"And what gave you the right to break into my **NATURAL HISTORY MUSEUM**, bring a long-extinct prehistoric animal back to life and then set it free?"

Elsie looked down at her feet.

"Well?" pressed the Queen.

"I don't know, ma'am," she replied.

"Well, you must have some sort of idea!"

The girl looked over to Dotty and Titch, who gave her nods of encouragement.

"Well, I, erm, I suppose…"

"Spit it out, child."

"Well, I, erm, I looked at Woolly…"

"I beg your pardon, who is Woolly?"

"Oh, that's the name I gave the mammoth, ma'am."

Queen Victoria gestured for the girl to continue. "Do carry on!"

"You see, Your Majesty, everyone was calling the mammoth a monster. But I looked on Woolly as a friend."

"A *friend*?" asked the Queen, incredulous.

"Yes. A friend, and like me she seemed lost without her mother and father. So I wanted to help her. Help her find her way home."

The Queen listened and nodded her head. "Looking at you, child, I take it you are an orphan?"

"Yes, ma'am," replied the girl. "I was left on the steps of an orphanage when I was a baby. I never knew me ma or pa."

The Queen leaned in. "Do you know if they're out there somewhere?"

"No, ma'am. I don't know if they're alive or dead."

This hit ᛞQueen Victoria like a thunderbolt. She was overcome with emotion. Her eyes closed, and she struggled for breath.

"Are you all right, Your Majesty?" asked Elsie. The little girl broke strict royal protocol and stepped forward to hold the old lady's hand.

ᛞQueen Victoria looked down at the grubby little hand holding hers. This simple act of kindness made a tear well in the old lady's eye.

"Here. Use my sleeve," said Elsie, offering up her arm to wipe the lady's face. This made the Queen smile.

"You, child, are a very special young lady," said ᛞQueen Victoria.

The little girl was rather taken aback. No one had ever told her that before.

ᛞQueen Victoria opened her arms, and folded Elsie into them. For a moment, these two people, separated by oceans of age, class and wealth, held each other tight.

It felt like all the world stopped.

"Thank you, child," said Queen Victoria. "I needed that."

"We both did."

"It's been so long since anyone has given this old lady a jolly good hug. Being the Queen, no one ever gives you one."

"Any time, Your Majesty."

The pair broke away from each other.

"Well..." began the Queen. "The whole world has been following this story in the newspapers. Myself included. Little did I know what was behind this extraordinary adventure. A deep and special friendship between an orphan girl and an innocent creature who just needed to find her way home."

Elsie nodded. "That's right, Your Majesty."

"This story has moved me. Not least because of all

your incredible bravery. So I declare that some prize-giving is in order. Munshi!"

"Yes, Your Majesty?" replied Abdul.

"Be a dear and bring me my box of medals…"

Chapter 76

❖

THE BRAVEST

The Chelsea Pensioners all stood proudly to attention.

"Now, I have something here for all of you," began the Queen, opening the shiny wooden box. "For my brave soldiers."

"And sailor!" prompted the admiral.

"Oh, and sailor. My apologies, Captain."

"Admiral!" corrected the old man grandly.

"Well, I asked my commander-in-chief to look into all of you. And I was told *you* never rose above the rank of captain."

The old soldiers all stared at him.

"Well, I, erm…" the man spluttered. "I think there was some sort of mix-up, Your Majesty."

"Really?" asked the brigadier. "I'm the confused one, not you!"

"Yes. I think when I was asked to leave the old sailors' home, and arrived at the Royal Hospital, all the old soldiers just started calling me 'Admiral'. Heaven knows why!"

There were murmurs of…

"You told us to call you that!"

"Big fat liar."

"I would love to stick that leg of yours where the sun don't shine!"

"Shark should have swallowed you whole!"

"Does this pub serve any food?"

"Did they, indeed?" The Queen was not convinced.
"Well, Captain, approach and collect your medal."

Nervously, the man limped over to the Queen.

DUFF! DUFF! DUFF!

As he saluted, Queen Victoria pinned the medal
to his chest. "As head of the British armed forces, I
hereby promote you to the rank of admiral, retired."

The newly appointed admiral turned round and
looked at the others smugly.

"Thank you, Your Majesty."

"Now get back to your place before I change my mind."

"Yes, of course, Your Majesty," he replied, limping as fast as his leg would carry him.

DUFF! DUFF! DUFF! DUFF! DUFF! DUFF!

One by one, she called all the old soldiers up, and pinned medals to their chests. Finally, it was Titch's turn. The soldier with just one lonely medal. The medal every soldier receives for service.

"Well, Private Thomas," began the Queen, "I have learned that your time in the military has not been distinguished. Despite serving in my army for over fifty years, you never rose beyond the rank of private. Somehow, despite being in some of the greatest battles in history, you've failed to fire even a single shot."

"I don't like loud bangs, Your Majesty."

"Over the years, Private Thomas, you have been mocked for your stature, but this extraordinary adventure has shown that you are a giant among men.

Do you know what this is?" she asked, dangling a cross-shaped medal.

Titch's eyes lit up. "Of course, ma'am. That is the highest honour a soldier can receive. The Victoria Cross."

"I rarely give these out. They only go to the bravest of soldiers. The Victoria Cross goes to you, Private 'Titch' Thomas, and you shall henceforth be known as Private 'Towering' Thomas."

The Queen bent down to pin the Victoria Cross to his chest. Titch looked at it, his eyes welling with tears.

"Thank you, Your Majesty."

As he turned round to face his comrades, they gave him an almighty "HURRAH!".

"This just proves, if ever there were any doubt, that heroes come in all shapes and sizes," said the Queen.

Private Thomas smiled proudly.

Then the Queen turned her attention to Elsie and Dotty. "Of course, heroism isn't something reserved for men only. Look at some of the great heroes of my reign. So many of them are women. Florence Nightingale,* Elizabeth Garrett Anderson** or Millicent Fawcett*** to name but a few. So I would like to award medals to you both as well. Dotty?"

The lady didn't move.

"DOTTY!"

"Me?" asked Dotty.

"Yes, you are called Dotty, aren't you?"

"Yes."

"Well, approach me, then, please."

"Now?"

"Yes. Now."

The lady curtsied with every step she took.

"Get a move on!" ordered the Queen.

"Apologies, jam."

Queen Victoria rolled her eyes, and went to pin the medal to Dotty's chest.

---

* *The founder of modern nursing, known as the Lady of the Lamp, who tended to wounded soldiers.*
** *The first woman to gain a licence to practise medicine.*
*** *She led the suffragist movement that campaigned for women's right to vote.*

"Let me help, Your Queen the Majesty," she said. All fingers and thumbs because of nerves, Dotty managed to stab herself with the pin.

"OW!"

"Are you all right?" asked the Queen.

"Yes. I'm fine. OUCH!"

"Are you sure?"

"I've just stabbed meself. But I'm fine. Really. I'm fine. OWEEE!"

Dotty then retreated, curtsying again with every step.

"Now, last but not least, Elsie!" said the Queen.

The girl curtsied respectfully, and she once again approached the old lady.

"Elsie, you have been the bravest of all. Living on the streets of London is brave enough, but you have been the driving force behind this extraordinary adventure. You did all this, not for yourself, not for personal gain, but to help, in your words, 'a friend'.

Elsie, you have shown uncommon valour."

Queen Victoria reached into her box for the final medal.

Then the girl spoke up.

"I'm sorry. I don't want to be rude and that. But I don't want a medal, ma'am."

A gasp echoed around the room.

Chapter 77

❖

NEVER FORGET

"You don't want a medal?" spluttered the Queen. "Everyone, but everyone, likes medals."

"All I want is for you to help orphans like me," replied Elsie.

The Queen thought for a moment. "Well, after all that's happened, I can hardly hurl you back out on to the streets of London, can I?"

Then a smile spread across the old lady's face. "All right. Young Elsie, why don't you come and live with me here at Buckingham Palace? You can keep me company in my old age."

"A splendid idea, Your Majesty!" remarked Abdul.

All eyes turned to the girl.

"I've got twenty-five friends," she replied.

"TWENTY-FIVE?" spluttered the Queen.

"Yes, they're all from the same orphanage as me. When I ran away, I promised I'd never forget them. And I haven't."

"What is the name of this orphanage?"

"**WORMLY HALL**: Home for Unwanted Children."

"Sounds frightful!"

"It is."

"And you ran away, Elsie?"

"I had to, Your Majesty. The lady who ran it used to beat me black and blue. I had to get out, or she would have killed me."

The Queen took a deep breath. She could barely believe what she was hearing, but she knew this girl was sincere.

"What is the name of this 'lady', if indeed the creature can be called that?"

"Mrs Curdle, Your Majesty."

"Hm. Munshi?"

"Yes, Your Majesty?" replied Abdul.

"Have this Mrs Curdle locked up in the Tower of London."

"With great pleasure, ma'am."

A huge smile spread over Elsie's face. This story did have a happy ending after all.

"Sometimes it's wonderful being Queen!" said the Queen. "And, Munshi?"

"Yes, Your Majesty?"

"Send a fleet of my carriages to collect those poor orphans, and bring them here to Buckingham Palace."

"All twenty-five of them, ma'am?"

The Queen gulped. "Yes. All twenty-five of them. We have the room!"

"At once, Your Majesty." With that, Abdul bowed and left.

"Of course, child, tonight is a very special night..." began the Queen.

"Is it?" asked Elsie. After being at sea for weeks, the girl had completely lost track of the date.

"Yes, my child. It's New Year's Eve. At midnight,

we welcome in a new century, as the year becomes 1900. Perhaps you and your twenty-five friends would like to join me for a midnight feast as we watch the fireworks?"

"Yes, please, Your Majesty."

"Splendid. I'll have my team of cooks lay on the feast!"

"I can't wait to see them all again, and tell them this incredible tale."

"I'm sure they've missed you, young lady."

Elsie smiled and turned to look at Dotty, before addressing the Queen again.

"Your Majesty?"

"Yes, Elsie?"

"Please can my friend Dotty come to the party tonight too? She's really looked after me. She has been like a grandma, actually. I would love to see in the new century with her."

The Queen took a deep breath. "Yes, all right. Dotty, you can come too, but please refrain from calling me 'ham'!"

"Ooh, thank you, jam!" replied the lady. "OOPS!"

Private Thomas was trying to catch Dotty's eye, to no avail. When that didn't work, he gave her a sharp poke with his elbow.

"What do you want? I'm talking to Queen Majesty herself, the ruler of everybody and everything!"

"Well, shouldn't the love of your life come too?"

"Who's that?"

"ME!"

"I'll ask," replied Dotty. She put her hand in the air. "Victoria the Majesty?"

"Yes?" replied the Queen uncertainly.

"Please could Towering Thomas come to the party?" she asked proudly.

"I won't take up too much space. You'll barely know I am there, Your Majesty," added the man.

Queen Victoria sighed loudly. "Well, I suppose there's always room for one more," she said.

"THANK YOU, MA'AM!" he replied.

Just then, the admiral popped his hand in the air.

"YES?" asked the Queen.

"Ma'am, if I could be so bold, I have been an extremely close friend of Private Thomas's for many a year…"

"No, you haven't!" he corrected.

"SHUT UP!" hissed the admiral. "And I would miss him terribly if I couldn't share this momentous night with him."

The old queen sighed. "All right!"

"Should I bring my own rum?"

"I am sure we have a barrel or two."

"Splendid! But what will everyone else drink?"

"Anyone else want to come to the party?" she asked.

All the old soldiers started nodding their heads enthusiastically and murmuring in agreement.

"Oh yes."

"Is it a buffet or a sit-down thing?"

"I can't stay too late. I really need to be back at the hospital before midnight."

"Yes, yes, yes, you can all come!" exclaimed the Queen. "Now, please, everyone leave immediately before I change my mind!"

You've never seen people exit a room so quickly.

Chapter 78

NOT ᴀ DAY
GOES BY

BOOM! WHIZZ! KABOOM!
Fireworks danced in the sky over London.
Those lucky enough to be on the top floor of
Buckingham Palace had the best view.

The elderly Queen was hosting quite a party. There
were the twenty-five WORMLY HALL orphans, all the
Chelsea Pensioners, Abdul, Dotty and, of course, the
guest of honour, Elsie.

Fittingly, a huge Victoria sponge cake was served. It was so big you could have dived into it, but it was demolished by the starving orphans in seconds.

By the fireplace, Private Thomas got down on one knee, to propose to his beloved.

"Dotty, will you marry me?"

"Where are you?" asked the lady.

"Here!"

Dotty looked down and spotted him. "Sorry, I didn't see you all the way down there."

"Dotty, will you marry me?"

"Ooh, I forgot to rinse me mops out!"

"DOTTY!" The little man was becoming irate now.

"WILL YOU MARRY ME?"

"There's no need to shout, dear. YES!"

The pair kissed as everyone around them clapped and cheered.

"HURRAH!"

BONG! *BONG!* *BONG!* *BONG!* *BONG!*
BONG! *BONG!* *BONG!*
BONG! *BONG!* *BONG!*

BONG!

Twelve bongs from Big Ben meant it was midnight.

1899 had ended, and 1900 had begun.

Everyone crossed arms, and Queen Victoria led the singing of "Auld Lang Syne".

♪ "SHOULD AULD ACQUAINTANCE BE FORGOT, ♫
AND NEVER BROUGHT TO MIND?
SHOULD AULD ACQUAINTANCE BE FORGOT,
AND AULD LANG SYNE?
♫ FOR AULD LANG SYNE, MY JO,
FOR AULD LANG SYNE. ♪
WE'LL TAK' A CUP O' KINDNESS YET,
♪ FOR AULD LANG SYNE." ♫

Robert Burns's words, and the mournful tune, made Elsie think about Woolly. She missed her friend terribly. As she sang, a tear rolled down her cheek, and she stole away to the far side of the room so nobody would see her. Elsie didn't want to spoil the celebration for everyone else.

Only the Queen saw that the girl was upset, and she broke away from the rest. The unlikely pair of friends found themselves alone in a corner, as fireworks illuminated them from the window.

"What's the matter, child?" asked the Queen softly as she placed her hand in Elsie's.

"The song. It just got me thinking about how much I miss Woolly."

"If truth be told, 'Auld Lang Syne' always makes me a little tearful too," replied Queen Victoria, her old eyes becoming misty. "It always makes me think of my darling husband, Prince Albert. I lost him thirty-eight years ago, but not a day goes by, not an hour, not a minute, when I don't think about him."

"It sounds like he was a very special man."

"Oh, he was, child, he was. The most perfect gentleman in all the world."

Elsie reached out her other hand to the old lady, who held it tight.

"See those fireworks, Elsie?"

"Yes, ma'am."

"That is how it felt in my heart every time my darling Albert entered the room."

"That's beautiful," murmured the girl.

"It was real. In the end, we've both loved, child – and been given love in return. What more can you ask of life?"

PRINCE ALBERT

"I suppose so," replied the girl.

"I know so. Elsie, you may look around this palace of mine, this country of mine, this empire of mine, which stretches to the four corners of the globe, and think I have everything. But believe me, child, you have nothing without love."

The Queen picked up a glass of champagne for herself, and handed a glass of lemonade to Elsie.

"To Albert," said Elsie.

"To Woolly," said the Queen.

CLINK!

The End

AFTERWORD

Learn More About Woolly Mammoths

The woolly mammoth roamed Asia, Europe and North America, and first appeared more than 400,000 years ago. They wouldn't have liked the Arctic much, because it consists entirely of ice so there is no food for them there. Even so, mammoths lived during the Ice Age and survived very harsh wintry conditions.

They were not unlike today's elephants, but with some differences – mainly their huge coat of thick, brown, woolly hair that kept them warm in the cold. They had two long pointy tusks, which they used to fend off hunters and predators. They also used their tusks to dig through the snowy ground as they searched for food and water.

Scientists believe woolly mammoths died out due to humans hunting them, or because of climate change at the end of the Ice Age, or both. The last known mammoths lived on Wrangel Island in the Arctic Ocean, around the same time that the Great Pyramid of Giza was built in Egypt about 4,000 years ago.

1. Woolly mammoths grew up to three metres tall, which is the height of two people standing on top of each other.

2. A fully grown male mammoth weighed around six tonnes. This is the weight of five Mini cars!

3. Their tusks could grow up to four metres long.

4. They were herbivores, which means they didn't eat meat. Their diet consisted of leaves, moss, berries, grass and twigs.

5. Woolly mammoths lived and travelled in large female-led family groups. This is also true of their relative, the modern elephant.

6. The average lifespan of a woolly mammoth is thought to be sixty years.

7. The best way to determine the age at which a mammoth died is by looking at its tusks. Age is shown by the number of rings on a cross-section of the tusk, but the early years wouldn't be accounted for, however, as these would show on the tip of the tusk, which usually wore away.

8. The tail and ears of woolly mammoths were actually quite small. This was to prevent heat loss from their bodies, and also stopped them from getting frostbite.

9. The first fully documented remains of a complete woolly mammoth skeleton were discovered in 1799 by a Siberian hunter, and were brought to a museum in Russia in 1806. Wilhelm Gottlieb Tilesius, using the skeleton of an Indian elephant as a guide, successfully reconstructed the mammoth except for one mistake – he put each tusk in the wrong socket, so that they turned outwards instead of inwards.

10. The youngest person to discover a woolly mammoth was an eleven-year-old Russian boy, Yevgeny Salinder. He came across the remains while out for a walk near his home in 2012. The mammoth was named "Zhenya" after Yevgeny's own nickname, but its official name is the "Sopkarginsky mammoth".

· ⚹ ·

NOTES ON THE REAL VICTORIAN WORLD

The Ice Monster is a story imagined by David Walliams so some of the extraordinary things you have just enjoyed reading might never have happened in real life. But the author has set his story in 1899 so you might be interested in learning some more facts about the real Victorian London!

THE NATURAL HISTORY MUSEUM

The Natural History Museum took seven years to build – and eventually opened in 1881. In 1899, when *The Ice Monster* is set, its official name was the British Museum (Natural History) although it was commonly known as the Natural History Museum. When the museum first opened its doors, you could find animal and human skeletons there, as well as collections of minerals and dried plants originally belonging to a scientist called Sir Hans Sloane. Sloane was also famous for having invented hot chocolate. The famous replica of the *Diplodocus* skeleton – or Dippy as you might know it – wasn't actually donated to the Natural History Museum until 1905! There were no life-sized models of whales on display in 1899, though there was a blue whale skeleton, and dioramas were later painted on to curved backgrounds.

THE ROYAL HOSPITAL CHELSEA

The Royal Hospital Chelsea is a retirement and nursing home for about 300 veterans of the British Army. It was founded in 1682 at a site by the Thames in Chelsea by King Charles II as a retreat for those who had served in the British Army. For special occasions and ceremonies, the residents, known as Chelsea Pensioners, wear distinctive scarlet coats and tricorne hats.

TANKS

The mammoth is cleverly disguised as a tank by Elsie and Dotty. In fact, tanks were actually not invented until 1915 and were first used in 1916 on the Western Front during the First World War.

THE ZEPPELIN

Zeppelins were a type of airship named after Count Ferdinand von Zeppelin, who came up with the idea in 1874. They had a fabric-covered, cigar-shaped rigid metal frame filled with bags of hydrogen gas and a cabin, called a gondola, hanging underneath. The first prototype flight did not, in fact, happen until 1900 in Germany, and it was only in 1910 that airships were flown commercially.

HMS *VICTORY*

HMS *Victory* was launched in 1765 and served in the American War of Independence and the French Revolutionary War. She is perhaps best known for her role as Lord Nelson's flagship at the Battle of Trafalgar in 1805. In 1899, when the story of *The Ice Monster* is set, HMS *Victory* was actually docked at Portsmouth, where she remains today.

HMS *ARGONAUT*

HMS *Argonaut* was an armoured cruiser in the British Royal Navy. Launched in 1898, she was commissioned for service in China in 1900. During the First World War, she was used as a hospital ship. She was sold and broken up in 1920.

QUEEN VICTORIA

Victoria became queen when she was just eighteen years old on 20 June 1837 and reigned for sixty-four years until she died in January 1901 at the age of eighty-one. At the time, this was the longest reign of any British queen or king. Victoria married Prince Albert of Saxe-Coburg and Gotha in 1840, and when he died she missed him very much and felt so sad that she rarely went out in public.

ABDUL KARIM

Queen Victoria was also the Empress of India. She asked that two Indian people be chosen to help prepare for celebrations of her Golden Jubilee, and in 1887 Mohammed Abdul Karim arrived at Windsor Castle. He taught Queen Victoria the Urdu language and became the first Indian clerk to attend to her personally.

LONDON WEATHER

Although the winter of 1899 was snowy, the River Thames did not freeze over. In fact, it had not actually frozen over since 1814, and since then has only frozen once, partially, in the winter of 1963.